PYROTECHNIC DEATH

A shockwave backblasted up the line, and the beam went rogue wild, out of control—a spectacular disaster that furnished Tracker with all the diversion he needed. Branton had one of the tubular shock sticks. He was swinging it across his body to get it into play, but Tracker got there first. Two of the guards rushed toward them.

Tracker wrestled with Branton's weapon hand, turning it so the muzzle was leveled at the onrushing pair. He got his finger on the control stud and thumbed it on. A fan-shaped jet of dirty blue-yellow energy vented from the weapon, scything the two guards. They burst into human torches, straw men tossed on a bonfire. Branton shrieked and clawed at Tracker's face . . .

The TRACKER series by Ron Stillman

TRACKER
TRACKER 2: GREEN LIGHTNING
TRACKER 3: BLOOD MONEY
TRACKER 4: BLACK PHANTOM
TRACKER 5: FIREKILL
TRACKER 6: DEATH HUNT
TRACKER 7: SHOCK TREATMENT

TRACKER

SHOCK TREATMENT

RON STILLMAN

DIAMOND BOOKS, NEW YORK

SHOCK TREATMENT

A Diamond Book / published by arrangement with the author

PRINTING HISTORY
Diamond edition / April 1992

ISBN: 1-55773-687-1

Diamond Books are published by The Berkley Publishing Group,
200 Madison Avenue, New York, New York 10016.
The name "DIAMOND" and its logo are trademarks
belonging to Charter Communications, Inc.

PRINTED IN THE UNITED STATES OF AMERICA

10 9 8 7 6 5 4 3 2 1

SHOCK TREATMENT

1.

A TRAIN STATION in Yellowfield, Colorado, was Shepperd Judd's jumping-off point into the Unknown.

He stood alone at the end of the platform, watching for the train. It had left Denver at nine-thirty that night. He should be able to see it any minute now. Yellowfield was thirty miles south of Denver, about midway between Mile High City and Colorado Springs. It sat on a broad flat plain fronting the eastern slopes of the Rocky Mountains. The railroad ran north–south, a highway ran east–west, and the town at the crossroads was Yellowfield.

It was a small town with a depot to match, a simple stone structure with a slanted roof which had been built around the turn of the century. It hadn't changed much since then. The light shining through its windows was warm and inviting, but Shepperd Judd preferred to do the rest of his waiting outside, where it was cold and dark and private.

He was running for his life with a suitcase full of payoff money. He had a gun in his pocket to protect both life and loot.

Inside the suitcase was seventy-five thousand dollars. That sounded like a lot of money but wasn't, not really. He was an accountant by trade and knew how quickly income becomes outgo. Seventy-five thousand was only the tip of the iceberg compared to what he'd made for his part in the Seven Cities mega-scam, but the bulk of the loot was locked up in long-term investments that he couldn't touch. Numbers were his stock in trade, but even he'd been caught short by the frightful speed with which Seven Cities' bubble had burst.

He'd amassed almost a quarter-million dollars worth of bribe money, but seventy-five thousand was all he could get his hands on at such short notice. His share of the take was chickenfeed. The big boys at the top, the chiefs of the money pirates, had made hundreds of millions.

What goes up must come down. Seven Cities' financial pyramid had collapsed. A large part of the economy of the entire Southwest was about to go under along with it. The magnitude of the crash was as yet undreamed of, even by the experts.

Regulators and investigators were starting to sniff around the edges of the mess. The money pirates weren't going to give up without a fight. Twelve potential witnesses who knew too much had died violently in the last six weeks. Some of them had known less about the inner workings of the scheme than Judd did.

Most of the deaths were "accidents" or "suicides." That's what the police called them, and they had no reason to suspect otherwise. Murder accounted for the rest. The victims were shot or stabbed in what looked like random street crimes. Empty wallets and purses were found near the bodies, supporting the robbery scenario. Random incidents of senseless violence, the police called them.

They didn't know that the single common denominator linking a dozen new corpses was the Seven Cities Investment and Development Fund Corporation. They had been killed so they couldn't talk.

Twelve corpses, eleven murders. One of the twelve had died from being struck by lightning. The odds against such a freakish finish were astronomical, but it seemed to have happened that way, according to the newspaper accounts Judd had read of it. Eyewitnesses reported seeing the victim actually being hit by a lightning bolt. That would have been tough to fake, thought Judd.

Fine. Eleven murders and one highly convenient Act of God. Convenient for the money pirates, that is.

Judd wasn't going to sit around waiting for the executioner.

He had gathered up what cash he could and taken it on the run. He was leaving behind a high-salaried post as a senior department head at the Denver-based home office of Baird and Lockride, one of the oldest and most respected accounting firms west of the Mississippi.

He was also leaving behind his wife of twenty-seven years and his three grown children. He wondered if the money pirates would take it out on his family, punishing them for his disappearing act. He hoped so. He hated their guts, all of them. Abandoning them forever helped to make up for the money he'd had to leave behind.

He'd done what he could to muddy his trail. After determining as best he could that he wasn't being followed, he'd driven his car to the airport and parked it in one of the long-term lots. Then he'd taken a cab to a bus stop outside the city limits. He took the bus to Yellowfield and went to the depot and bought a ticket for the southbound train. It was all part of a ruse to throw off the hunters with a false trail.

1So far everything had gone according to plan. The money pirates had a network of agents covering the Southwest, but they couldn't cover it all, and Yellowfield was the kind of place that fell through the holes in their spy net. A small town in the middle of nowhere, the perfect springboard for a leap into limbo.

It wouldn't be long now. A light flickered into being in the north, the headlight of an oncoming train. It was on time, give or take a few minutes. Strange to think that the trains might stop rolling in the near future! The collapse of Seven Cities would have a paralyzing effect on commerce and industry in this state and its neighbors. But the trains would keep running long enough for him to make his getaway. After that, he didn't give a damn what happened to them. In fact, the greater the chaos, the better his chances of escape.

A gust of cold wind buffeted him. The winds blew down from the mountains, through the passes of the front range of the Rockies, which walled off the horizon in the western distance. Flatlands stretched eastward from the foothills for hundreds of miles.

Yellowfield was a cluster of lights on a sea of black darkness.

The depot was on the western outskirts of town. The only lights burning on the main drag in the center of town were the streetlights. Stores and shops were dark, closed.

What activity there was took place at the truck stop on the east side of town, where there were fuel pumps and a diner. A police car was parked in the lot, facing the highway, its headlights dark. Not much traffic passed through town, just some big-rig trucks and a few cars. None came near the depot.

He could hear the train whistle now. It sounded good to him: escape, freedom, triumph.

A strip of ground a hundred yards or so wide separated the railroad line from the town, isolating the depot. It was bare of snow. The weeds were dry from the long winter which was nearing its end. They rustled in the wind.

No, it wasn't the wind. Someone was moving through the fields, trampling the dried weeds underfoot. The footsteps sounded close.

Judd looked around but didn't see anyone. The footsteps had stopped. Suddenly it seemed to be a bad idea to be standing alone out there at the end of the platform. An icy blast of wind brought tears to his eyes. When he blinked them away, a figure came into view. One instant it wasn't there and the next instant it was. It hadn't appeared by magic, it had merely stepped out from behind the cover of a pile of railroad ties stacked a stone's throw away from the depot. It must have been hiding behind them.

It looked human. Weird, but human. Its manlike form was encased in a bulky headset and thickly padded uniform. The outfit resembled a space suit or, more accurately, a deep-sea diver's pressure suit and helmet. The sight was so bizarre that it froze Judd in place.

The figure cradled a bulky object in both arms. The device was roughly the size and shape of an old-fashioned metal milk can. Starlight gleamed on it. Flanges and coils and boxlike housings bristled from its tubular body.

It was heavy. Its operator wore a shoulder sling to help support its weight. A wide-mouthed funnel protruded from one end of it. It was pointed at Judd.

The operator's gauntleted hand flicked some switches on a

panel on one side of the device. A hum filled the air, as if a giant transformer had been suddenly switched on. A flickering blue glow outlined the operator and the device. It shone brighter as the humming deepened. It was the hum of power, electromagnetic power. Tiny blue-white lightnings danced across the device. Tongues of electric fire licked out from the operator's form.

There was a smell of ozone. Air crackled with static electricity. Sparks flew from the steel rails of the tracks. The fillings in Judd's mouth buzzed like a dentist's drill was working on them. The rails shone with blue foxfire. So did the power lines strung alongside the tracks. The depot lights dimmed. So did the lights of town.

A blue-white disc of light blazed into being at the bottom of the wide-mouthed funnel. It was bright, dwarfing the headlight of the train hurtling across the middle distance. So bright that it hurt Judd's eyes, making him look away. That broke the spell of the paralysis that had gripped him. He turned and ran, the gun in his pocket forgotten.

The operator triggered his device. The blue-white disc became a sphere, a three-dimensional globe of scintillating light. The fireball was launched and flew after Judd. It sailed above the tracks in a low arc, closing with its human target.

Judd's hair stood on end. His tooth fillings rattled so hard that he thought it would split his head. His wire-rim glasses were suddenly outlined with blue fire. Shrieking, he grabbed at them to tear them off, but the fireball got him first. The instant it touched him there was a blinding flash, followed by a deafening clap of manmade thunder.

The town of Yellowfield blacked out, stilled by a complete power failure.

"I hurl my thunderbolts like Zeus," the weapon operator said. He was long gone before the lights came back on.

The people in the depot were the first to discover the body. It was charred and smoking, burned black from head to toe. The eyeballs had been cooked until they popped. A pair of wire-rim spectacles had been turned into molten metal and glass, branded deep into the carbonized skull. His fillings were melted,too.

The suitcase with the money inside it had been burned to a crisp.

The best explanation that any of the baffled onlookers could come up with was that the victim had been struck by lightning. But there wasn't a cloud in the sky.

Shepperd Judd was dead, killed not by an Act of God but by a mad genius who thought he was God.

Dr. Shock.

2.

TRACKER CAME TO Mountain City on a mid-April morning.

A mile higher than Denver, Mountain City sat astride one of the key passes through the Continental Divide. It lay at the hub of the Kettle, a bowl-shaped rock-ringed high mountain valley. Mineral-rich mining country. Including outlying districts, Mountain City's population numbered close to forty thousand, making it one of the bigger cities in the state of Colorado.

It was a beautiful morning. The sun was shining and birds sang in the trees.

Tracker parked his pickup truck on a side street a few blocks away from the municipal plaza where the courthouse was located. He didn't want to park too close to the courthouse in case there was a riot. He left his gun inside the vehicle and started walking.

He was a big man, rangy, athletic. His hair was black; his features were strong, cleanly made. He wore a pair of what could have been ski goggles or sunglasses. Their design was simple, striking, stark. The visor curved across the middle of his face like a black plastic blindfold. The exotic eyewear would have looked at home on the expensive slopes of Aspen. It was the only touch of flamboyance about the man. Apart from the visor, he seemed little different from other men in Mountain City, just bigger and more intense.

The municipal plaza was a centrally located square where official business was transacted. City Hall was there and the county courthouse and police headquarters and other civic administrative buildings. The older edifices were made of stone and the newer ones of steel and glass. The plaza was a rectangle whose long sides ran north–south. A park with a war monument in it lay at the center.

Tracker entered the plaza at its southern end, where there was a cluster of commercial buildings. Most of them were empty and dark, even though it was a business day. The front windows of the Columbine Bank had been broken and were now boarded over with sheets of plywood. Its padlocked doors were marked with the seal of the state police. Shards of broken glass lined the gutter.

The courthouse rose on a hill at the opposite end of the plaza with its front facing south. Tracker crossed the park to reach it.

The park was in a sorry state. Waste baskets were filled to overflowing, spilling litter that the wind had scattered throughout the space. The statue atop the war monument was so fouled with bird droppings that it looked like a slimy ghost. The pathways were dirty, unswept.

Tracker stepped on a sheet of newspaper which lay on the ground. LOCAL REALTOR KILLED BY LIGHTNING, read the headline, but he took no notice of it. He had other things on his mind.

He had to stop Jeff Purdy before he killed somebody. He had to find him first. When Tracker set out to find someone, he usually did. He was a supreme manhunter, among other things.

So far there was no sign of Jeff, or even of his car, but that didn't matter. A good hunter anticipates the actions of his quarry. Jeff would go to the courthouse. He might be there already.

Tracker paused at the edge of the park to scan the scene. The courthouse was on the other side of the street. It was a fine example of Greek Revival architecture from the 1920s. Stone pillars upheld a jutting portico high above the arched main entrance. It looked like a temple, a temple of law and order.

Under the portico was a statue of Justice. It was the traditional representation of Justice as a blindfolded woman in long flowing robes holding aloft the Scales of Balance and armed with the Sword of Truth.

Justice was blind. So was Tracker.

• • •

Major Nathaniel Hawthorne Tracker was a former radar officer who was officially retired from the United States Air Force due to disability. A head-on collision caused by a drunk driver had blinded him, killing the sight in his eyes. Anyone else would have been condemned to live the rest of his life in perpetual darkness, but not Tracker.

Above all else he was a thinker, a scientist-inventor in the mold of such greats as Morse, Edison, Marconi, and Tesla. His specialty was optical electronics. His goal was to make the invisible visible, to "see" beyond the narrow limits of human eyesight deep into the hidden realms of the electro-magnetic spectrum. He probed the secrets of infrared and ultraviolet wavelengths. He held patents for important inventions involving radar and sonar technology, thermal imaging, and computerized tracking systems.

His work had vital national security applications. His clearance grade was ultra–top secret. He was part of the shadow world that exists at the highest levels of military and civilian intelligence agencies and experimental weapons research and development teams. They were the brain trust of America's techno-war establishment.

After the accident, his eyes were dead but not his brain. He had a lot of time to think while recuperating in a hospital bed. He conceived a bold plan, a daring gamble against the darkness. His premise was that high-technology hardware could make a blind man see. He volunteered to be the human guinea pig for the experiment.

The proposal generated immediate interest. A group in the hush-hush National Security Agency, the Big Eye and Ear whose mission is to monitor the global communications net, offered to fund and develop the project as its sole sponsor. Chiefs at the military's Defense Intelligence Agency argued that they should be in charge. After all, Major Tracker had been on active duty in the Air Force at the time of his accident. The covert action branch of the Special Operations Directorate of the CIA scrambled for a piece of the action. The President said that it sounded like a pretty risky idea to him but that sometimes risk was a part of exploring the frontiers of science.

Long months of intensive research preceded the moment of truth. Early on, the project's parameters leaped far beyond Tracker's initial concept. He'd tackled the problem solely in terms of the video-sonic hardware. But *he* was the software. He—his body, his flesh and blood, his nervous system. Teams of medical specialists labored to perfect the bionics of the man-machine fusion.

Finally there came a day when the last test runs were successfully completed and there was nothing left to do but install the prototype system in its human host, Tracker.

The operation was performed in the maximum security wing of a hospital on a restricted military base somewhere in Virginia. Oxygen tanks and pumps and life-support systems crowded against banks of computerized electronics equipment in the oval operating theater. Medics and scientists alike were outfitted in sterile masks, rubber gloves, and surgical gowns.

Tracker was prepared for surgery and wheeled into the operation room. His head had been shaved as bald as an egg. He went under anesthesia. The darkness lost its focus as the gas took effect. Voices and sounds echoed as if they came from somewhere a great distance away. . . .

Automated overhead video cameras documented every detail of the marathon fifteen-hour session. Success or failure, there'd be a complete record of it. A blueprint for the next attempt or a roadmap showing where this one had gone wrong.

A surgeon fainted from stress in the sixth hour, and a technician monitoring a life-computer screen had to be relieved from duty due to burnout in the eleventh.

. . . Tracker woke in darkness.

Inwardly he steeled himself against bitter disappointment. He silently vowed to perfect the apparatus no matter what it took. But the experiment wasn't a failure. The video-sonic system had not been switched on yet. The doctors had wanted to wait until he was fully conscious.

"I'm ready now," Tracker said. "Switch it on."

They did. There was a pause in which nothing happened. In real time the interval lasted only a fraction of a second, but to Tracker the tortuous suspense seemed to stretch out for centuries.

Suddenly there came a hum of power, so soft and low that Tracker could barely hear it, perhaps he imagined it—

And then there was light!

• • •

That was over two years ago. Since then the video-sonic system had been constantly upgraded. The prototype was crude compared to the hardware he now wore, the Mark III third generation series. Multi-millions of dollars worth of state-of-the-art cybernetic implants interfaced with his nervous system. They made him a one-man mobile electronic eavesdropping center, able to transmit, receive, and detect signals and communications across the EMG spectrum. A unique human asset in the twilight world of espionage.

From time to time he was called on to perform certain secret missions on behalf of his country. Missions of paramount importance to the survival of the United States. He'd undertaken such assignments in the past, both at home and abroad. "Undertaken"—that's the word, since his objectives were rarely achieved without heavy casualties. Enemy casualties mostly, but not always. Civilians got caught in the crossfire of covert wars, too. Governments must take actions they dare not admit to in public.

Tracker had not come to Mountain City on a military intelligence mission. He was on his own, on a mission of mercy to stop a good man from becoming a killer and probably getting himself killed. Jeff Purdy was that man and he was a friend. Tracker meant to save him, and a man who has conquered blindness is unlikely to be thwarted by lesser obstacles.

Standing at the park's edge facing the courthouse, he said, "ATR—Search."

He spoke in a whisper that was softer than a sigh. It was loud enough to be received by a miniaturized bone-phone transceiver implanted in the skull a few inches behind his ear. The unit then relayed the command to the sub-micro computer system in Tracker's eye visor.

Tracker viewed the plaza scene and "saw" it in a way unlike any other ever witnessed by the eyes of man.

His "eyes" weren't—weren't eyes, that is. His dead eyeballs had been surgically removed on the operating table of that Virginia hospital and replaced with artificial orbs virtually indistinguishable from the real thing. Not glass eyes; glass was too breakable. The ersatz eyes were made of ultra-tough, durable ceramo-plastic material. Only a detailed opthalmologic examination could tell them apart from a genuine human eye.

Amazing though they were, those fake eyes were only the

housings for even greater wonders. Each orb contained a fully operational mini-video camera of extraordinary accuracy and power. Fiber-optic leads from the cameras fed into bio-mesh nerve-set membranes lining the backs of the eye sockets. The bionic membranes transformed the video feed signals into electrical impulses that were then transmitted through the organic optic nerves into the visual centers of the brain. The binocular camera eyes created a stereoscopic imaging effect, allowing Tracker to see objects in depth.

That was the basic self-contained mechanism that gave eyesight to the blind. Add-on options and augmentations greatly expanded its video-sonic power. The micro-computerized optivisor was one such force multiplier. There were others. The most powerful force of all was the genius of the mind that had conceived of such scientific marvels and brought them into being.

Now Tracker's video eyes focused on a wide-angle image of the north plaza. The picture was crystal clear. He saw it in black and white. The problem of seeing in color was still a long way off from being solved. No matter. He could see "colors" and energy patterns invisible to the naked eye.

He couldn't see Jeff Purdy, though. Not yet.

A crowd of several hundred people was gathered at the foot of the courthouse steps. That was as close as the police would let them get. The crowd was angry, and it wouldn't take much to turn it into a mob. It was made up of local citizens from all walks of life: city folk and their country cousins, male and female, young and old. There were office workers, town merchants, ranchers, miners, secretaries, clerks, and others, plus plenty of kids and senior citizens. They radiated hostility.

A platoon of state police stood ready to keep the peace. They guarded the courthouse's strategic access points, staring stone-faced over the heads of the citizens who shouted abuse at them. They weren't equipped with such anti-riot gear as batons and Plexiglass shields. That might be a mistake, thought Tracker.

Where were the Mountain City cops? Tracker didn't see them at first. Then he saw a group of them bunched together on the platform at the top of the courthouse stairs. They stood off by themselves at one end, pointedly distancing themselves from the state police. Apparently there was no love lost between the city and state lawmen.

The crowd consisted of several hundred individuals. Was Jeff Purdy one of them? A face-by-face search would take a long time, too long. Tracker speeded up the process by using the ATR/Search program.

ATR—shorthand for Automatic Target Recognizer. That was one of the functions built into his computerized opti-visor. The target was Jeff Purdy.

Earlier that day Mary Ellen Purdy, Jeff's wife, had given Tracker a recent photograph of her husband. Unknown to her, his video eyes had scanned the picture and stored the information as binary pulses in the micro-computer's memory bank. His vocal command labeled it as the prime target of an ATR/Search program.

When the ATR was on it scanned every face that flashed across Tracker's field of vision, comparing them with its stored image of Jeff Purdy. And it did so in nano-seconds. If there should be a match between face and image, in other words if it found Jeff, it would lock onto its human target, pinpointing his location and vector. Tracker didn't have to think about it; the process was automatic. If the target appeared on his view screens, no matter how briefly, the ATR would find it.

But Jeff must not have been in the crowd because the ATR didn't find him. It didn't spot his car anywhere in the immediate vicinity, either. Tracker had input Jeff's car as a secondary target, since the ATR had multi-search capacity. Tracker had learned the car's make, color, and licence plate number and verbally input the information into the ATR's parameters.

Jeff had a good head start and he was smart, too. Smart enough to figure out a way inside the courthouse where *his* target awaited. He could even have entered the courtroom legitimately as a spectator if he'd arrived early enough. The trial wasn't closed to the public. Every seat in the courtroom was filled, and hundreds more would-be observers had been turned away. They made up the crowd clustered outside. They wanted in but the state police said no. The situation was at an impasse so far but that could change quickly.

A hot dog vendor had his wagon set up at the northeast corner of the park. He sold hot coffee and cold soda, too. He was stocky with curly black hair and a bushy gray-flecked mustache. Pinned to the shoulder strap of a soiled bib apron was a nametag that said: HI I'M GENE.

Tracker said, "How's business?"

"Lousy. So are the franks, for that matter," Gene said.

"You won't sell many of them that way."

"Mister, I ain't been selling them any way. Pretty soon I'll be out of business like the rest of this town."

"Maybe it'll pick up. Lots of folks out here today," Tracker said, indicating the courthouse crowd.

"They don't want food, they want Brady Sullivan," Gene said. "Besides, they ain't got no money. Brady stole it all. That's why they're out there hollering for his blood."

"I heard something about that. He's a bank president, isn't he?"

"He was. He used to be the biggest man in Mountain City. Now he's washed up, and the town is, too. The crook!"

"Takes all kinds, I guess," Tracker said.

"Eh? What's that? You'll have to speak up, mister, I can't hear you so good over those jerks."

By "those jerks," Gene meant a small but noisy group of protesters walking a picket line across the street directly opposite from him. There were about two dozen of them grouped on the concrete apron at the bottom of the courthouse hill. They stood well apart from the angry crowd on the steps. Two of them, a man and a woman, sat on folding chairs around a card table that had been set up on the sidewalk. Piles of pamphlets and newsletters were stacked on the table and placards hung down from it.

The others shuffled around in a small circle, carrying picket signs and chanting slogans. The men wore jackets and ties and the women wore business suits, but despite that there was a touch of shabbiness about them. Their garments were mostly cheap and overdue for a cleaning. There were plenty of dingy grayish-white shirts, frayed cuffs, tattered hems, and down-at-the-heels shoes.

The outfits mirrored their owners. Although the picketers were in their thirties and forties, they seemed much older. Prematurely aged. Their skin had a white waxy pallor that comes from too much time spent under indoor lights, away from the sun. Black rings of fatigue circled their eyes. But the eyes themselves blazed bright with the fanaticism of true believers.

"Hey hey, ho ho, Brady's got our dough," they chanted while marching in a circle. "Hey hey, ho ho, Brady's got to go!"

"Loud bunch," Tracker said.

"They're kooks. Creeps. Moxies, they're called," Gene said. "It's like a cult or something. They're followers of that weirdo egghead who got kicked out of the government for saying people are like bugs."

"Moxon. Owen Moxon."

"Yeah, Moxon."

"What do they want?"

"Brady clipped their dough like he did everybody else's. They sure got a big hate for him. They've been out here protesting since Day One of the trial. Get here first and leave last and make lots of noise in between. They're lousy for business, too. They scare away the customers."

Tracker crossed the street to the courthouse side.

He swung wide to avoid the demonstrators but took a closer look at them anyway. The placards hanging down the sides of the card table looked like campaign posters. Larger than life–sized photo portraits of Owen Moxon glared out from every one of them. A balding middle-aged man with an impressive double-domed cranium and tight crabbed features. Pinpoint eyes stared out from behind thick-lensed black-rimmed glasses. His head was too big for his neck and shoulders.

The posters were headlined:

STARWARD BOUND

WITH THE HIGHER ECHELON

Higher Echelon was the name of Moxon's group. Its branches were spread throughout the U.S. but its headquarters was located right here in Colorado, in Boulder, not far from Denver.

Ascension was the group's self-published monthly magazine, a slickly produced showcase to promote Moxon's ideas. Piles of the latest issue were heaped high on the table. Moxon's face was on the cover. Other pieces of Moxonite literature were also available.

Seated at the table was a sour-faced man and a leathery

woman with a clownish orange perm. The woman saw Tracker glance at the display and took him for a prospect. She pasted a smile on her face and opened her mouth to speak, but Tracker moved away fast before she could start in on her pitch.

The protesters kept on marching in a circle, shuffling and chanting with no sign of a letup. There was something stiff about them, mechanical, robotic. Tracker was reminded of similar demonstrations he'd seen staged behind the Iron Curtain in East Europe in the bad old pre-Glasnost days. Those were usually KGB propaganda fests designed to show support for the regime in power. Moxon was no Marxist, but his demonstration had a similar air of artificiality.

Higher Echelon was a classic personality cult. Ugly rumors hung over it like a black cloud. Defectors told of brainwashing, mind control, coercion, violence. Tracker didn't know if the rumors were true or false. Maybe someday he'd find out.

But that was a subject for future investigation. Right now he had to find Jeff Purdy.

The crowd on the courthouse steps couldn't have been more different from Moxon's minions. It was big, raw, rowdy, and boiling with potential chaos. It had surged forward so that its front edge just lapped the platform at the top of the stairs. Tracker had to get through that mass of people. There was no way to avoid them, not if he wanted to get where he was going. He took a deep breath and plunged in.

He pushed into the fringes of the crowd and bulled his way inward. He wasn't shy about it, either. He moved forward, snaking through the gaps. When there weren't any gaps he opened some up through deft use of his shoulders, elbows, and knees.

The crowd parted for him. Angry shouts and curses marked his passage. Kicks and punches were thrown at him but somehow none of them ever connected. He seemed to have an ability to put himself where the blows weren't. A silver-haired old lady stabbed at him with a rolled-up umbrella. The thrust speared empty air where Tracker had been an eye-blink earlier. A beefy miner who didn't like being shoved swung a big fist at the back of Tracker's head, where the base of the skull joins the neck. It would have dropped him if it had landed. It couldn't miss, but it did. At the last possible instant before impact, Tracker's head bobbed suddenly to the side, causing the punch to pass harmlessly over his shoulder.

The miner stumbled, off-balance. By the time he'd recovered, Tracker was out of his reach.

"That guy must have eyes in the back of his head!" the miner said.

He didn't know how right he was.

No one could sneak up on Tracker or surprise him from behind. He was protected by omni-directional ultrasonics.

It was a function of the computerized opti-visor. It worked on the same principle as a bat's sonar. Transceivers set into the visor's earpieces emitted ultrasonic pulses too high-pitched for human hearing to detect. The sound waves bounced off solid objects such as fists and umbrellas. The echoes were picked up by the transceivers, creating a three-dimensional sonic picture. When an object came within close proximity of Tracker, it set off a beeping in the bone-phones implanted behind his ears. The closer the object, the louder and more frequent the beeping.

Open space loomed as Tracker neared the front of the crowd. A few more steps and shoves brought him through into the clear of the platform at the top of the stairs.

Two state troopers moved to intercept him. Nametags identified them as TAYLOR and VOSS.

Tracker took a slim eelskin card case out of his pocket. Many cards had been issued to him by various high-level government agencies, identifying him as one empowered to command the complete cooperation of those authorities to whom the card was presented.

He left the federally issued cards untouched in the case and presented one that had been signed by the governor of the state of Colorado—the troopers' boss.

The troopers let him pass.

3.

STONE PILLARS ROSE up on either side of Tracker as he crossed to the courthouse entrance. Some members of the crowd tried to do the same, but they didn't have courtesy cards from the governor. The troopers pushed them back, not gently.

The Mountain City cops stayed put in their corner of the portico. They wanted to sit this one out if they could.

A few of them glanced at Tracker as he passed by. Their eyes held only indifference, boredom.

The state police was a military-style organization of law enforcement professionals. The Mountain City Police Department was a different proposition, if the cops in front of the courthouse typified the rest of the force. Their uniforms were blazoned with MCPD shoulder patches and bright shiny badges. Apart from that, they looked more like hoods than police officers.

Mountain City was a tough town. It needed tough cops, and these men looked tough. Not one of them was less than six feet tall; all were packed with plenty of muscle. Hardnoses. Their weapons weren't regulation-issue: .357 and .44 revolvers and 9mm and .45 semiautomatic pistols, big guns with plenty of man-stopping power. They stood their post like they were loafing at a pool hall. They smoked, spat, scratched, and laughed.

"Nice," Tracker said to himself.

He smiled as he passed the statue of Blind Justice. "You and me both, baby," he said.

"Excuse me?"

The speaker was a woman who sat on a stone bench behind the back of the statue. Her voice was rich, resonant. She was a strikingly attractive brunette in her early thirties. Her hair was pulled back and tied in a knot at the back of her head. She wore glasses and little makeup. She didn't need makeup, not when she was naturally endowed with arched black brows, wide dark eyes, strong cheekbones, and red lips.

He was guessing about the red lips, since his video eyes were colorblind. But he could see that her lips were full and moist and provocatively shaped.

The rest of her was provocatively shaped, too. Nature hadn't skimped on the anatomical endowments. The plain, almost severe charcoal-gray jacket and matching skirt that she wore covered but could not conceal her statuesque physique.

A man hovered around behind her, but Tracker didn't take much notice of him.

She said, "I'm sorry, I thought you were speaking to me."

"Uh, no. Sorry," Tracker said, "I was just talking to myself."

"That's supposed to be one of the first signs of insanity."

The other man put his hand on the brunette's shoulder, leaned forward, and said, "Is he bothering you, Anne?"

"Not yet."

"Some other time, maybe," Tracker said.

"Quien sabe?" Anne said, shrugging. "Who knows?"

Her escort was peeved. "Listen, you—" he began, but Tracker moved on before he could say more.

When he thought Tracker was out of earshot, the escort said, "Somebody ought to teach that wiseguy a lesson in manners!"

"Who's going to do it, Branton? You?"

"Think I couldn't?"

"I'd like to see you try."

"Don't underestimate me, Anne. You've never seen me in action."

"Thank God for that."

"You don't think much of me, do you?"

"I try not to think of you at all, except in the line of duty."

"I must be doing something right or I wouldn't have this job."

"You won't have a job if you don't get your hand off my shoulder. You won't have a hand, either," Anne said.

Branton's hand leaped off her as if scalded. He looked sick.

"You know I can do it, too. Or have it done," she said.

"Hey, Anne, I was just kidding around, I didn't mean anything by it—"

"Shut up. You don't have the faintest idea who that man is, do you?"

"No. Who is he?"

"The X-factor. The unforeseen variable that changes the equation."

"I don't get it."

"Does the name 'Tracker' mean anything to you, Branton?"

"That was Tracker?"

"Yes."

Branton took a few steps forward, craning his neck to try and catch sight of Tracker. But Tracker was already inside the courthouse, lost from view.

"So that's Tracker!" Branton said. "From all I've heard about him, I thought he'd be a lot bigger. He didn't look so tough."

"A number of dead men found out otherwise."

"And some dead women, too, according to the reports I read."

"That's true. Tracker wouldn't hesitate to kill a woman if he thought she was an enemy."

"I like that. It puts your neck on the chopping block right along with mine, Anne. Gives us an incentive to work together."

"How charmingly you put things."

"It can't be coincidence that Tracker shows up here today. Where does he fit into the picture?"

"We'd better find out."

The troopers guarding the courthouse's front entrance had seen Tracker pass through the line. They let him enter the building unchallenged. He went through a high arched portal into a marble-floored lobby.

His video eyes automatically adjusted to the transition from the sunny outdoors to the dimmer artificially lit interior. A key feature of his video-sonic system was a feedback effect that constantly responded to changes in his immediate environment. Built-in safety circuits guarded him from being blinded by too bright a light or deafened by too loud a sound.

Court was in session. The courtroom's dark wood double

doors were closed. A pair of troopers stood with their backs to the doors.

A few dozen people stood waiting in the lobby. They included courthouse staffers and a large number of mid-level bureaucrats whose departments had an interest in the outcome of today's hearings. A few second-string reporters were scribbling on notepads. If they had been first-string, they would have been in the courtroom.

Jeff Purdy was not among those outside the courtroom.

There was disorder in the court. The hearing had reached some kind of a conclusion. That it was not a happy one for the spectators was obvious from the uproar with which they greeted the decision. The hundreds in the packed courtroom buzzed like bees whose honey has just been stolen. Their outrage came through the closed doors loud and clear.

"Uh-oh," said someone in the lobby.

The judge pounded his gavel until the outburst quieted down to sullen mutterings. The hearing was adjourned.

The dark doors opened and a man rushed out of the courtroom well in advance of everyone else. He was a grizzled old-timer with long gray hair and a straggly white beard that made him look like a billy goat. He must have been a local character since he was immediately recognized by some in the lobby.

A reporter shouted, "How did the judge rule, Dusty?"

The oldster said, "Brady got bail!"

The news set off a hubbub in the lobby. It was small compared to the one still going on in the courtroom.

Dusty was eager to spread the bad news. He hurried outside, nimbly avoiding a trooper who tried to stop him. He was small and surprisingly agile. He went to the far end of the portico and stood where the crowd on the courthouse steps could see him.

"Brady got bail! The judge's letting him walk! Brady got bail!"

Dusty spread the word with the enthusiasm of a town crier. The troopers closed in on him, more determinedly now, but too late. The damage had already been done.

"He paid that bail with our money, the crook!" bawled an angry voice from the crowd.

"He'll skip out with the rest and leave us holding the bag!" said another.

Dusty disappeared inside a ring of troopers.

"Look! They got Dusty!"

"Let him alone, he didn't do nothing!"

"Yeah, he's not the crook!"

"The big bullies, pushing around a little old man. It's a disgrace!"

"Ya lousy cops!"

The crowd surged forward. Those in the rear pushed the hardest. The human tide spilled over the top step and rolled forward across the platform. The troopers formed a line to contain it, a thin line with too many gaps. There was a lot of pushing and shoving, but the citizens weren't worked up enough yet to start throwing punches at the troopers.

The Mountain City cops stayed aloof from the conflict. They withdrew into an even tighter knot and looked the other way.

"What's with you guys?" a trooper said. "Give us a hand before this bunch runs wild!"

"You state boys are supposed to be in charge, so take charge," a city cop said.

"I don't believe it. You're just going to stand by and do nothing?"

"When this is all over we've got to live with these people. You don't."

"Thanks for nothing."

"You're welcome," another city cop said. Some of them laughed.

Inside the courthouse the scene was equally chaotic. Officers tried vainly to clear the courtroom, which was still in an uproar. People milled aimlessly throughout the main floor of the building. Some tried to enter the courtroom, others tried to leave it. They blocked the doors and each other and the result was a near-total impasse.

"Brady got bail." That meant that he would be leaving with his entourage instead of going back to jail. It was a sure bet that he wouldn't go by way of the front entrance, not with that mob out there. For his own safety he would be taken out of the courtroom through the door to the judge's chambers, then hustled out a back exit of the building and away.

By that line of reasoning, the back of the building was where Tracker should be, too. It was a long way off and a mass of people stood between him and it.

Opposite the courtroom doors on the other side of the lobby, an archway opened onto a flight of stairs. He bulled his way through a mass of humanity to reach it. It was like plowing through a wall of mud.

All resistance ceased the instant he entered the stairwell. It was empty, except for him. There were no police guards to bar the way. If there had been any here in the first place, they had all gone elsewhere when the trouble began.

Tracker climbed two flights of stairs to the second-floor landing. He sent an ultrasonic pulse ahead of him as a scout. Returning echoes reflected off walls, recessed doorways, overhead lighting fixtures. Inanimate objects all. No humans.

Tracker stepped into the hall, a long corridor that ran the length of the building. There were offices on either side of it. They were all closed. All nonessential personnel had been furloughed for the day in anticipation of potentially dangerous demonstrations.

The opposite end of the corridor was some distance away. Tracker squinted to get a better look at it. Sensitive neuromuscular receptors linked the muscles surrounding his "eyes" to the video orbs set in the sockets. When a normally sighted person wants to see something far away, he squints. When Tracker squinted, his eye muscles activated zoom lenses in his video eyes.

The far end of the hall rushed toward him even though he was standing still. That was the effect of the zoom. It could be dizzying if done too fast.

The opposite end of the corridor was now revealed on his scanners as clearly as if he stood but a few feet away from it. All clear.

Tracker widened his eyes, as if expressing surprise. This triggered the zoom effect in reverse. The scene now seemed to rush away from him. He halted the process by relaxing his eye muscles to their normal position. This stabilized his vision to the electro-optical equivalent of 20/20 eyesight.

He went down the long hall. An alert observer might have noticed that Tracker walked with his feet turned out. This gait was a by-product of years of intensive martial arts training. The front two knuckles of each hand bore calluses as big as marbles. The hand edges were rough as unplaned boards.

He was light on his feet. His passage was virtually noiseless, except for the faint sound of his shoe leather scuffing the linoleum floor.

At the end of the hall was another stairwell. Tracker stepped out cautiously on the landing. A flight of stairs descended to a mid-level landing, then a second stairway continued the descent to the first floor. Windows inset in the shaft walls supplied light and air. They opened on a view of the parking lot behind the back of the courthouse. The lot was restricted to the authorized vehicles of court officers, police, and a select number of civilians who'd been given special permits to park there.

A black stretch limousine stood not far from the courthouse's rear exit, idling its engine. A uniformed driver sat waiting behind the wheel. Four men were grouped around the car, each of them keeping watch in a different direction. They were private security guards in plainclothes, working for Brady Sullivan, no doubt.

Tracker stood to one side of the window frame, sticking his head slightly around the corner so he could see without being seen. A subtle change in position brought a previously unseen section of the parking lot into view.

A set of neon-green crosshairs suddenly flashed into being before his eyes. It was a video effect projected on the inner screens of his dark glasses, his computerized opti-visor. The polycarbonate lenses worked on the same principle as one-way glass. Tracker saw the image on the inner side of the lenses, but the visor's exterior remained opaque and unchanged, betraying no sign of the cybernetic processes at work within.

The Automatic Target Recognizer was working now. It had been working since he first activated it earlier by verbal command but only in its passive search mode. Now it had found what it was searching for and gone into its active phase of alerting him.

The green phosphor crosshairs were wire-thin so as not to obstruct his vision. They zeroed in on a target in the parking lot and locked onto it, pinpointing its location.

A rush of hope surged through Tracker at the thought that he had found Jeff Purdy. It was stifled by the computer message that appeared at the bottom of his eyescreen:

SECONDARY TARGET FOUND.

"Secondary Target." That was Jeff's car, and sure enough, that's what the ATR/Search program had found. Tracker zoomed in for a closer look at the dark late-model sedan in his sights. The license plate numbers matched. It was Jeff's car, all right.

Jeff was nowhere to be seen.

Tracker subvocalized a command: "IR mode on."

His angle of view stayed the same but the spectrum of light changed. It switched to "IR"—infrared mode, another function of the opti-visor.

The electro-optical system was now a thermal imager. It saw heat, not light. It operated similarly to the guidance system of a heat-seeking missile.

The world of the infrared was a ghostly one. Tracker saw it in black and white and shades of gray. All objects radiate heat in greater or lesser degree. The hotter an object, the brighter it appeared on Tracker's screens. The cooler it was, the darker it appeared.

Human bodies are organic furnaces with a temperature of 98.6 degrees. They showed up as featureless, white man-shaped blobs on the IR screen. Machinery generates much heat. Engine shapes blazed brightly inside the cars and trucks that they powered. Tracker could see their intense heat signatures glowing through the walls of their engine compartments. Solid walls were not necessarily a barrier to seeing things in infrared.

Even engines that have been turned off continue to radiate heat for some time after they've ceased operation. Tracker could see them, too, if the time frame was not too great. Sometimes he could even detect ghostly after-images of vehicles that had already left the scene if they had put out enough heat in one place for a sufficient time. It was a world of multiple exposures, phantasmic images, and shimmering blobs of raw heat-energy.

The engine in Jeff Purdy's car was still warm. It didn't shine as brightly as those in moving cars or as dimly as those in cars that had been parked in the restricted lot since early morning.

The car was empty. Tracker had played a longshot hunch that Jeff might be hiding inside it, ducked below the dashboard out of sight, lying in wait for Brady Sullivan. The hunch didn't pan out. Jeff wasn't there. His heat signature would have been visible to Tracker clear through the car body walls. It couldn't hide from his infrared sensors.

"IR off," Tracker subvocalized.

His vision switched back to "normal," to the video version of the human-visible light spectrum.

How had Jeff managed to get his car into the courthouse parking lot with its reserved spaces? Admittance was restricted, or supposed to be. Gate guards would decide who got in and who didn't. Jeff had no credentials and no City Hall clout. According to his wife, he had looked and acted like a wild man the last time she had seen him. That was earlier this morning, when Jeff had stormed out of the house with murder in his heart.

No gate guard with an ounce of brains would grant admittance to a wild-eyed, obviously distraught man with no legitimate reason for parking in the courthouse lot in the first place. Any policeman worth his salt would have taken a close look indeed at such a suspicious character. Of course, that's what could have happened. Police might have questioned Jeff, not liked his answers, searched him, arrested him, and taken him away.

The flaw in that theory was the presence of Jeff's car in the lot. The cops weren't going to waste a precious reserved parking slot on the car of an arrested suspect. They would have left the car on the side of the road, out of the way, until a tow truck arrived to haul it down to the police garage.

So how did the car get in the lot?

Something was wrong, off-kilter. A Mountain City police car with two cops in it sat idling in the lot not far from the black limo. Another was stationed outside the gate. No state troopers were present. They were all trying to contain the disturbance in front of the courthouse. It hadn't reached the back of the building yet.

There was nothing about the scene to suggest that it was a facade masking a sinister setup. Except for Jeff's car being where it shouldn't be.

A sudden impulse prompted him to store up certain bits of information for future reference.

"Input—on."

His video eyes were micro-miniaturized TV cameras. The Input program made a permanent record of what they saw, storing it in photonic patterns on fiber-optic filaments in the visor's computerized circuitry. He could record images, store them indefinitely, and call them up when necessary. An invaluable tool for a scientist, detective, or spy—or for a man like Tracker, who was all three rolled into one.

He scanned the scene, recording it. When his video-eyed gaze fell on the big black car, he said, "Acquire vehicle."

The "Acquire" command flagged the car with an identifying marker which allowed it to be inserted as a potential target in the ATR/Search program, among other things. Tracker had a feeling that it might come in handy.

"Input—off."

Jeff wasn't a killer. That was what made him so dangerous now. He was a decent law-abiding citizen who paid his taxes and minded his own business but was always ready to extend a helping hand to those less fortunate than himself. He had a wife and kids. He was the president and CEO of Purdy Precision Machine Tool Company.

The business had been started forty years ago by his father, Bill Purdy. Old Bill had long since retired from active management and was content to let Jeff run the show. Father and son held the majority shares, preventing hostile takeovers by outside interests. The company was small, smart, successful. It manufactured intricate measuring devices, custom-made to order. Exqusitely precise instruments, accurate to the last decimal point. They were built at a high-tech automated factory with low overhead and less than a hundred employees. The factory was in Dumont, a suburb of Mountain City.

The company funds had been kept in the Colombine Bank. When the bank went bust, the company was bankrupted overnight, wiped out. Old Bill suffered a stroke when he heard the bad news. His condition was critical and he wasn't expected to live.

Tracker had come on the scene not long after that. His arrival was no coincidence. He planned to investigate the woes of Mountain City in general and of the Purdys in particular.

He had driven out to Jeff's house. It was a handsome place on a hill where Dumont's elite made their homes.

Mary Ellen Purdy was frantic and the kids were screaming and crying. When she finally recognized him through her tears, her eyes lit up like she was seeing an angel. It made Tracker uncomfortable, but what could he do?

"Thank God it's you, Natty. You've got to stop him before it's too late!"

"What's wrong?"

"Jeff's got a gun. He's going to kill Brady Sullivan!"

4.

VOICES FROM BELOW ended Tracker's recollection of the chain of events leading up to the current crisis.

"They're getting ready to bring Brady out. Everything okay at this end, Miller?"

"All clear so far, Sarge."

"Good. Lt. Boyd wants Brady out of here before the dopes out front figure out where he is. Go outside and tell the boys to get ready. We're gonna whisk him out the back door and into his car. After that he can look out for his own neck."

Miller was a uniformed cop who was guarding the first floor landing of the back stairs. Securing access. Sarge was his boss. Neither of them thought to look upward into the stairwell, and even if they had, they wouldn't have seen Tracker. He crouched behind a bannister, hidden from their view.

Following orders, Miller went outside to pass the word about the banker's imminent departure. Sarge took his place. He stood facing the hall with his back to the stairwell.

After a moment, some people approached from another part of the building. Not Brady Sullivan and his entourage, but a group of citizens who had wandered to the back of the courthouse.

Sarge said, "This area is off limits. Go back the way you came—*pronto*!"

The intruders were not minded to obey.

"You deaf or something? Beat it before I have all of you run in."

Somebody shouted something that wasn't nice.

"What did you say? *What?!* I'll kick your ass, you prick!" Sarge said, barreling down the hall after the offender.

Other cops grabbed the enraged sergeant and held him back. One said, "Take it easy."

"Let me at him, let me at him!"

"Cool it, Sarge."

"Lt. Boyd's coming, Sarge," said another.

"Boyd?"

"Him and all the rest of them."

Sarge's face was red and swollen. Veins as big as fingers stood out throbbing on both temples. He visibly mastered himself, stifling his rage.

"All right, all right, let go. I'm okay now."

"You sure, Sarge?"

"Just do it, damn it."

One of the cops who wasn't restraining Sarge went over to the man whose remark had triggered the outburst. The man was frozen with shock, fear.

"You'll get out of here fast if you know what's good for you," the cop said.

The citizens ran in the opposite direction with the frightened man leading the pack.

Sarge shook off their hands. He took off his cap and pushed back his mussed hair before putting the cap in place. Breath hissed out of him like steam.

The long central corridor branched off into a T-shape at the rear of the courthouse. The stairwell was opposite the corridor. One branch of the top bar of the "T" was lined by offices on both sides and had a utility closet at its far end. The other branch bordered the back of the main courtroom on one side and a row of offices on the other side. All the offices in the rear of the courthouse were dark, silent.

Waves of noise from the riot in the front of the building rose and fell like a stormy sea.

The intruders who'd been chased away spread the word that something was afoot at the back of the courthouse. Something big, or else the cops wouldn't have chased them away. What were they trying to hide?

A lot of people suddenly wanted to find out the answer to that question.

"Here comes some more of them, Sarge," a cop said.

"That does it," Sarge said. "Use your nightsticks if you have to, but hold the line. Nobody gets through, understand? Nobody!"

"There's reporters around."

"So?"

"Some of them have camcorders. I don't want to see myself busting heads on the ten o'clock news."

Sarge lowered his voice. "Go after the video cameras first," he said. "Don't bust them up, just take the tape out of them and get rid of it. Well, bust them up if you want, but take the tape out first.

"Now hop to it and push those slobs back. And keep them back! I don't want them to even see Brady. Bust heads if you got to, but keep them back!"

The cops formed up in a line, standing shoulder to shoulder with nightsticks at the ready. They sealed off the corridor, then advanced, wading into the oncoming human tide. That was a lucky break for Tracker, the first he'd had in a while. Taking advantage of the diversion, he slipped noiselessly downstairs to the first-floor landing.

The cops in the corridor had their backs turned to Tracker. Sarge had gone into the hall behind the back of the courtroom. He couldn't see Tracker from where he stood, either.

A door opened in the back of the courtroom. Before anyone could emerge, Sarge said, "Here they come!" He said it loudly, but not shouting. Why had he said it at all? He hadn't been speaking to his men. They were around the corner and down the central corridor, too far away to have heard Sarge's announcement. He stood alone in what he thought was an empty hallway. Maybe he was talking to himself.

A rush of people came pouring out of the rear exit of the courtroom. The hall started filling up fast with uniformed city cops, plainclothes detectives, court officers, lawyers and their assistants, others. Among them was Brady Sullivan.

Brady Sullivan was a zombie in a good suit. The living ghost of what had once been a sleekly prosperous power broker. He was just going through the motions now. He had a fresh haircut and a shave but he looked sick. He'd lost weight recently, too much of it too fast, and now gray folds of flesh hung down from his face. He was brittle, shaky, shifty-eyed.

A man stood beside the banker, propping him up. He held him cop-style, with one hand clutching the other's arm above the elbow. A classic come-along.

The steerer was big, beefy. His hair was snow white. It was thick, full, and styled into a pompadour. His bushy eyebrows were all white, too. He had a face like the butt end of a ham. His gray and black–checked suit looked as expensive as Brady Sullivan's, but he wore his better. Its custom-tailoring minimized but could not hide his big gut and the big gun holstered under his left arm. He said, "All set, Sgt. Maggard?"

"Ready when you are, Lieutenant."

"Right. Let's move out."

Sgt. Maggard—that was "Sarge."

The other was Lieutenant Boyd, the officer in charge. A big bull of a man who looked like he'd come up the hard way and had enjoyed every inch of the climb.

Maggard was the ape to Boyd's bull. He was squat and wide-built with tremendous upper body development. Younger than Boyd, closer to Tracker's own age, an adult male in his vigorous prime.

Boyd started forward, sweeping the banker along with him. Brady Sullivan's feet barely touched the floor. The others followed close behind.

A door suddenly swung open on the side of the hallway opposite the courtroom wall. The door of a dark office which stood roughly midway between the oncoming Brady Sullivan and the stairwell. A man lunged wildly through the doorway into the hall.

PRIMARY TARGET FOUND

The words flashed into being at the bottom of Tracker's inner view screen. The ATR/Search program had finally located its prime target, Jeff Purdy.

Jeff came hurtling out of the office with a gun in his hand. He skittered to a stop in the middle of the hall. He was face to face with Brady Sullivan at pointblank range.

Shots were fired. They ripped through the banker's chest, shredding his heart and lungs.

Sgt. Maggard stood behind Jeff. Maggard was fast. He had

his gun out and working a split-second after the first burst of gunfire. He emptied it into Jeff's back.

Muzzle flares flashed like lightning, reports crashed like thunder. A bullet blew apart the back of Jeff's skull, disintegrating it into a geyser of blood, brains, and bones. He bounced off the walls and hit the floor. He was dead before any of the other cops had even drawn their guns.

Brady Sullivan was dead, too.

The shooting stopped.

The world stood still for a blessed instant, a pause between heartbeats. Then came chaos. Shouts, screams, pandemonium. Some people dove for cover. Others were frozen in place, their mental gears jammed. Police guns came out now, pointing in as many different directions as there were cops. One of the banker's bodyguards belatedly searched for his shoulder-holstered gun and was almost shot by a skittish cop.

Was the violence over or was this only a lull before the next attack? No one knew. Gunsmoke clouded the scene, adding to the confusion. There was a lot of blood on the floor. Some cops circled Jeff's body, closing in on it with drawn guns. Jeff lay face down in the center of a fast-spreading pool of red. The back of his head was gone. He still held a gun. The cops approached him warily, ready to shoot if he so much as twitched. They were taking no chances.

PRIMARY TARGET FOUND—PRIMARY TARGET FOUND—PRIMARY TARGET FOUND—

The message kept flashing on Tracker's screen. The ATR/Search program was still in operation, locked in on Jeff. Green phosphor crosshairs remained targeted on him, pinpointing the location of his corpse.

"End Search," Tracker said.

The ATR/Search program terminated. Target crosshairs and flashing status read-out message strip vanished into nothingness.

Lt. Boyd stood with his back against the wall. His front was speckled with red. He was mopping ruby droplets off his face with a handkerchief.

Another detective said, "You okay, Lieutenant?"

"Yeah."

"You've got blood on you."

"It's not mine. It's Brady's."

"You're lucky."

"The suit's ruined, though. You can never get those bloodstains out. I'll have to throw it away. And you call that lucky?"

"Well, yeah. I mean, it's just a suit, right?"

"You wouldn't say that if you knew how much it cost," Boyd said. "Oh, well, let's get to work."

Brady Sullivan did not die alone and unmourned. A woman sat on the floor with her legs folded under her, cradling the banker's head in her lap. His chest was a raw ruin but his face was untouched. There was a strong family resemblance between the dead man and the woman. Tracker thought she might be his grown daughter. She kept screaming for somebody to do something.

A man stood nearby with his legs bent and a hand pressed to the wall for support. A fussy little man with curly hair parted in the middle and a fussy little mustache. He wore a pale yellow suit and a blue shirt and a bow tie. His eyes were staring pits of horror.

Boyd said to him, "You're one of the lawyers, right?"

"This is awful . . . the most terrible thing," the fussy man said.

"Sure, sure. But you're one of Brady's people, and I need your help. So snap out of it, huh?"

"I—I'm going to be sick."

"Well, don't do it here. This is a crime scene now and I don't want you fouling it up."

The fussy man's face was turning green. The longer he stared at the corpses the greener it got, but he couldn't bring himself to look away.

"There's a toilet in the judge's chambers, chum," the other detective suggested helpfully. "If you hurry, you might make it in time."

The fussy man bobbed his head in grateful acknowledgement. He turned and scuttled down the hall, bent nearly double, holding one hand clamped across his mouth.

"What did you tell him that for, Monty? There's no toilet in the judge's chambers."

"I figure that's the judge's problem, not mine."

Boyd said, "Keep thinking like that and you're a cinch for promotion."

"Thanks, Lieutenant."

There was a mood of barely contained hilarity which is often found among those who have come through unscathed from a brush with violent death.

Boyd approached a tightly coiffed woman in a business suit. She held a slim leather legal portfolio pressed against her chest. She was part of the team of the banker's defense lawyers. Boyd said to her, "You look like you've got some sense, counselor. Why don't you give Brady's daughter a hand? She could use some help."

"I—I'll see what I can do, Lieutenant."

"Thanks. Get her out of here, huh? She shouldn't have to see any more of this." When the lawyer was out of earshot, Boyd said in an aside to Monty, "Besides, that screaming is driving me nuts."

"Looks like they're taking her away now. Tough break, seeing her old man get gunned down like that."

"Saves the taxpayers a bundle, though. C'mon, let's go take a look at the killer."

Boyd halted when the toes of his wingtipped shoes were a few inches away from the edge of a pool of blood.

Monty said, "Is he dead?"

"With his brains smeared all over the ceiling? What do you think?" said a uniformed cop.

"That smart mouth of yours is going to get you reassigned to dogcatching detail one of these days, Kelly."

"He was just talking, Monty. He didn't mean nothing by it," Maggard said.

"Always looking out for your boys, eh, Sarge?"

"You know me, Monty."

"All right. I'll let it ride this one time."

"You're a pal."

Boyd said, "Nice shooting, Sarge."

"I just happened to be in the right place at the right time."

"Don't be so modest. There could be a citation in it for you. Who knows how many others might have been killed if you hadn't stopped this nut in time?"

"Just doing my duty."

"And a damned fine job you did of it, too."

"Well, thanks," Maggard said.

Boyd placed a foot on the wrist of Jeff's gun hand and stepped down hard. Dead fingers opened, unclenching the fist.

Boyd bent over and used his handkerchief to pick up the gun. Lifting it by the barrel, he dropped it into the handkerchief and wrapped it up.

"The murder weapon," he said. "Important evidence. The coroner will want this in a hurry. I'd better deliver it myself. The rest of you men carry on until I get back. You know what to do."

A permanent record of the scene was being stored in the memory of Tracker's micro-circuitry. An audio-visual record. The visual feed was supplied by Tracker's optics. Sound was picked up by a pair of directional mini-microphones built into the framework of the visor. The filament-shaped, wire-thin mini-mikes were inset lengthwise in the earpieces.

Tracker had started inputing a few seconds after the last shot had been fired in the double killing. Grief and rage over the death of a friend were luxuries to be indulged in later. He had a job to do now, a job only he could do, one that the high-tech hardware in his head had been created for.

A subvocal command switched on the Input program. From then on, until further notice, it would transcribe what he saw and heard into the cybernetic memory bank. The storage capacity was limited and there was a danger of overloading it by continuous use. But the critical threshold was still far-off.

Jeff was dead. He was a good man who had set himself on the road to destruction when he picked up a gun in anger.

But he wasn't a killer.

He hadn't murdered Brady Sullivan.

He hadn't even fired his gun!

That was Tracker's belief. He'd been watching Jeff while the banker was cut down, and he was sure that his friend hadn't fired a shot. But he didn't have to trust his memory of the lightning-fast explosion of violence. He had something better.

He switched his vision band to IR—infrared.

The hall was filled with glowing ghosts, the heat signatures of human bodies as depicted by the thermal imaging system. The two dead men blazed as brightly as the living, for now. Soon that would change and they would dim out as their corpses cooled.

The overhead lights were fluorescents but they radiated plenty of heat anyway. They showed up as a crisp band of cool brightness running along the ceiling. Ceiling, walls, and floor were strangely insubstantial, misty.

Maggard's gun was a revolver-shaped blob of white-hot incandescence. That was only natural. Gunfire generates a lot of heat.

But Jeff's gun was cool and dim. Because it hadn't been fired at all!

The evidence was on the record now. The Input program had continued to function non-stop when the infrared vision was switched on, recording the feed off the thermal imager.

If Jeff hadn't killed Brady Sullivan, who had?

Tracker turned to the office from which Jeff had so suddenly emerged. The door was closed. It had been open when Jeff came flying into the hall. "Flying" was the word. Like he'd been pushed. Who pushed him? The same person who'd closed the door from the inside.

The *real* killer.

Jeff was only a pawn, a patsy. The fall guy in a brutal frame-up. The real killer must have been waiting with him inside the dark office, waiting for Brady Sullivan. Maybe Jeff thought he was a friend, an ally. When the banker showed, the killer shoved Jeff out into the hall and opened fire, making his kill. It all happened so fast that the cops thought Jeff did it and shot him down.

The killer who made such a hit must be a cool-nerved pro and cunning, too. And one thing more: he couldn't do it alone. The killing, yes, but not the frame. For the frame to stick he needed someone on the inside.

Tracker's heat-seeking sensors probed at the office's door and walls. Solid objects could block his infrared vision. The more there was of the object, the less heat he could "see" through it.

Door and walls now became semitransparent to him, letting him see into the office. The vision was murky, unclear. He could distinguish light from shadow but just barely. He saw shapes.

He didn't see the killer. That didn't mean he wasn't still lurking somewhere inside, it just meant that Tracker didn't see him. But he did see a definite point of brightness hovering at waist-height somewhere in the office's inner recesses.

Maybe it was the murder gun. It would be hot, too, like Maggard's gun was.

Tracker switched from infrared back to normal vision.

There was a tingling sensation behind the backs of both eyes. It was a warning sign that the electro-optical system was nearing the limits of its power supply due to the demands he was making of it. It was an early warning sign, that tingling. He was still well within the safety zone. But if he ignored it for too long, the tingle would become an itch. The itch would start to burn. Presently he would feel as if his optic nerves were on fire, lancing his brain with hot needles.

Then the auto-safety overrides would shut the system down, leaving him stone blind until the indicators all dropped out of the danger zone.

Now the tingling stopped when he switched off the infrared. Operating IR and Input at the same time drained a lot of power.

Maybe the killer was still in the office, maybe not. It looked like the murder gun was there, though. It was possible but unlikely that the killer had escaped through the window. He'd prefer a more discreet exit. Perhaps he'd used a connecting door to enter an adjacent office. That was a better bet. It was beyond his IR range so he didn't strain the system by switching back to that mode.

He'd have liked nothing better than to go charging after the killer but that wouldn't be smart. In the aftermath of the double homicide, the cops all had their guns out and were ready to shoot anything that moved fast and looked wrong. So Tracker stayed put for the moment, though it was torture to do so. He wanted to get his hands on that killer!

It was a solid frame but it had a loophole. The tricky part was with the guns. Somewhere along the line the guns had to be switched. The murder gun had to be substituted for Jeff's gun and Jeff's gun had to be gotten rid of. That would tie everything up into a neat package which could be marked "case closed".

That's why the murder gun had been left behind, to help make the switch. The killer had done his part. Now it was up to the inside man. He had to make the switch.

When Lt. Boyd picked up Jeff's gun, Tracker knew who the inside man was.

5.

Tracker said, "Stop."

The cops stopped what they were doing and looked at him.

Detective Monty was long, lean, and dry, with a face like crumpled paper. He said, "What's griping you, chum?"

"A man with a gun is hiding in one of these offices," Tracker said. "He shot Sullivan from inside that office. You couldn't see him from where you were standing, but I could. I think he's still in there, or maybe the room next door."

"A nut," Monty said. "Get him out of here, we've got work to do."

"I can prove what I'm saying. Check the gun belonging to the man you thought was the killer. You'll find that it hasn't been fired!"

"Sure, sure," Boyd said soothingly. "And it's made out of green cheese, too."

He winked broadly at the others, as if to suggest that he was humoring a lunatic.

"You were probably in too much of a hurry to give the weapon more than a glance. Take another look and you'll see right away that it hasn't fired a shot," Tracker said. His careful phrasing still left Boyd an out. It assumed that his failure to notice the obvious was a simple oversight caused by the pressure of his many responsibilities. It gave him an easy way out, provided he wasn't in too deep.

Boyd's grin was unshaken. "You bet I was in a hurry," he

said. "The man in the moon wants to see this evidence right away. He's my boss and he doesn't like to be kept waiting, see?"

"So that's how you want to play it," Tracker said.

"I don't follow you there, son."

Kelly said to Tracker. "Who're you?"

"A nut. Get rid of him," Monty said.

"He looks like an accomplice to me," Boyd said, his grin gone. "We'd better take him in for questioning."

The atmosphere became charged with tension. The cops looked at Tracker in a new way, sizing him up to see how he could be taken. The lower-ranking cops, the ones who would have to actually make the arrest, set their jaws and started to move in.

Tracker said, "If there's one honest man among you, check the gun and you'll know what I'm saying is true."

"Careful, he looks desperate," Boyd said.

It was Maggard who made the play.

"He's got a gun!" he shouted, reaching for his own.

It was an old trick used by crooked cops to eliminate troublesome characters. Shoot first and claim later that the suspect was reaching for a weapon. Savvy rogue cops sometimes carried a "throwdown gun," a small cheap handgun without a history, which they could plant on a corpse to prove a case of legitimate self-defense.

Tracker had wondered where Maggard fit in the picture. Was he just a quick-triggered cop or was he part of the frame? Now he knew that Maggard was dirty all the way.

Tracker's blistering side kick was a blur of fast motion. His foot left the floor in a high hurtling arc. Maggard caught a brief glimpse of the ridged sole of Tracker's booted foot before the edge of it slammed into his mouth with pile-driver force. It knocked Maggard out. The impact rocked him backward, sending him crashing into the other cops, jamming them up in a tangle of bodies. It was the power of Tae Kwon Do, the Korean martial art of unarmed combat. The practitioner's body is the weapon. The technique includes fighting from deep-rooted stances with powerful kicks and blocks. Tracker was a master of the art.

He'd taken a long gamble in playing by the rules instead of going after the killer by himself. If it had worked, he could have cleared Jeff's name and nabbed the real killer with one stroke. But he hadn't reckoned on the corruption of the Mountain City cops. He hadn't trusted them, either, and that's why he was ready to explode into action when trouble came.

He took particular pleasure in the satisfying crunch of his foot impacting Maggard's mouth. It wasn't a killing blow; his stance hadn't been deeply rooted enough for that, but it would put Maggard out of commission for some time to come.

Tracker had launched the kick from a side stance. No sooner had it been delivered than he turned his head in the opposite direction and charged a door. The door of the office that had held Jeff and the killer. It was locked. The killer had thought of that.

The main group of cops were untangling themselves from Maggard. Boyd backed up, clawing at a .38 Detective Special in a clip-on holster at his side.

Tracker darted a quick glance at him. Boyd was out of kicking range. Tracker's hand crashed into the door panel just above the knob. He hit it with his palm-heel, a short sharp jab. The blow broke the lock, snapping it out of the doorframe.

Kelly had his gun out.

"Shoot!" Boyd said, swinging his own gun into line.

Tracker ducked, halving his height. His rearward leg swung in a swift wide arc just above the floor in a sweeping motion. His foot hooked Kelly's ankle with such force that it knocked his footing right out from under him. Kelly threw his arms up as he fell back off-balance. His finger jerked the trigger, sending a shot crashing into one of the overhead light fixtures. The long tube lights exploded in a shower of glass.

A bullet blasted a hole in the doorframe, spraying Tracker with splinters and powdered plaster. Boyd's bullet. He dove into the office before Boyd could shoot again.

It was a headfirst dive that propelled him deep into the darkened office. He slid across the floor on his belly, then rolled to one side.

More bullets. They missed.

The office was divided into sections. Just inside the door was a reception area. The receptionist's desk was off to one side. A water cooler stood opposite it. The reception area was partitioned off from the rest of the space. The partition stretched across the width of the office. It was eight feet high. The first five feet was solid metal and the top three feet was thick pebbled glass. There was a door in the center of the divider, which was now closed.

Tracker rolled behind the cover of the receptionist's desk just as a figure filled the doorway and opened fire. He was just shooting, he hadn't seen Tracker yet. Some light shone in through the open doorway but not enough to dispel the gloom.

Tracker crouched behind the desk. His fingers closed on a clump of wires. They connected a desktop phone to the wall outlet. He yanked hard, tearing the cords loose from the wall.

The cop heard the noise and snapped a shot in Tracker's direction, hitting the desk. The cop craned his neck, looking for a better shot.

Leaving some play in the cord, Tracker whipped the phone off the desk and whirled it overhead like a bolo. The cop shot, missed.

Tracker didn't. He released the cord and sent the heavy phone flying. The missile hurtled straight on target. The cop shouted, raising his arms to protect his head at the last second. The phone hit him square in the middle, in the pit of his stomach. He folded up and fell backward, blocking the door.

There was a typewriter on the desk, too, an electronic model with word-processing functions. Tracker picked it up with both hands and heaved it like a shot put. It sailed across the office and into the water cooler.

There was a tremendous crash. The cooler toppled, smashing the glass water bottle into fragments. The diversion drew police bullets, as Tracker had planned.

Uncoiling, he leaped on top of the desk and used it as a launching pad to propel himself over the top of the partition and into the inner office.

He hit the floor, rolling to absorb the impact and to present a moving target. He fetched up against a desk, slamming his shoulder against it. He got his feet under him and hunkered down with his knees bent and hooked his hands against the underside of the desk.

He lifted, straightening his legs. Muscles bunched in his shoulders, veins stood out on his face. He heaved harder and the desk upended, standing first on its side, then crashing to the floor on its back. It had fallen so that it now blocked the inner office door.

Tracker had hoped to retrieve the murder gun, but there was

no time for that now. He was only a few seconds ahead of the police, and that was the margin of safety that was keeping him alive.

The desk had overturned with a tremendous crash. The noise must have panicked whoever was in the adjoining office. Bullets came tearing through the connecting door. They'd have killed anyone standing in front of it.

The gunfire slowed the cops down. They hadn't expected it. They thought Tracker was unarmed—dangerous, but unarmed. The shots in the inner office weren't aimed at them, but they didn't know that. They broke their charge and ducked for cover before returning fire.

From the adjoining office came the sound of breaking glass. Windows were being smashed, and not by gunfire. They were being shattered deliberately.

The killer was in the next room and he was trying to escape! It had to be him. There wasn't any sense in the cops firing through the door and then breaking the window, but it made perfect sense if it was the killer being stampeded into a getaway.

Tracker dove across the floor, tumbling into a forward somersault. He got his feet under him and jumped, launching a flying front snap kick at the connecting door.

It imploded, jackknifing as if it were hinged in the middle. The two halves fell into the room.

The killer stood on the windowsill, preparing to jump. He'd ripped down the curtains and used a chair to shatter the window pane. He was kicking the last shards out of the bottom of the frame when Tracker kicked in the door.

The killer was a dark-haired man, a stranger. Snarling, he popped a shot at Tracker but missed. Tracker had already dodged out of the line of fire.

The killer fired again, out of desperation or sheer rage, then jumped out the window.

Tracker rushed into the office, to the window. The ground lay ten feet below. The killer crouched there on his hands and knees, trying to shake off the effect of a hard fall.

He glanced over his shoulder and saw Tracker outlined in the window he'd just jumped out of. He had a square-shaped face with dark narrow eyes, a flattened nose, and a tight-lipped mouth. He wore quiet, unobtrusive clothes. He was dressed like a lawyer but looked like a hood.

When he saw Tracker, he spun around and fired; even as his finger jerked the trigger he saw Tracker move out of the way.

The killer had had enough. Besides, his shot had drawn attention. He got to his feet, staggered, broke into a run. He must have been hurt by the fall because he hobbled.

"Gotcha!" Tracker said.

He'd captured the killer on the Input program. He had a permanent record of his face, height, weight, even the gun he used. That wasn't the murder gun, of course; that weapon was hidden somewhere in the other office. It didn't matter. Tracker had the killer's image etched on his circuits and that was enough.

He'd also tagged him on the Acquire program. That would allow him to be designated as a target in the ATR/Search program. The killer didn't know it, but he was already trapped in a cybernetic web.

The manhunt's success was contingent on Tracker's staying alive. That was by no means certain.

The cops rushed in. Tracker jumped out the window.

The ground rushed up to meet him. It was soft from recent rains. He hit the ground, rolled. It was an easy jump for one like himself, who had spent hundreds of hours being bounced around on the training mats of the dojo by experts.

He tumbled to the side, trying to get outside the line of fire of the cops who would be at the window any second now. As his roll lost momentum, he bounced to his feet, faked right, and moved left. He crouched low, almost double, offering the smallest target possible.

The office he had just exited was near the northeast corner of the courthouse, well to the right of the rear exit. It was on the ground floor but the hill at the back of the building had been cut away and leveled off to create the parking lot. That accounted for the ten-foot drop.

Most of the flattened hilltop was taken up by the enclosed lot. Tracker—and the killer—had landed outside the fence on a narrow strip of lawn. Beyond the edges of the manmade plateau, the north side of Courthouse Hill sloped gently downward for a hundred yards or so to end at the first cross street. A long curving driveway connected the lot with the street.

The killing of Brady Sullivan and his presumed assailant had created confusion among the cops and the banker's bodyguards waiting in the lot. They went into the building, toward the crime scene. The second round of shooting, set off by Tracker's escape, had confused those on the edges of the scene. They took cover, holding their fire until they knew who to shoot at.

The killer half-ran, half-staggered to the edge of the grassy strip. He was favoring his right leg, which had been injured in the jump. His face was intent and he was breathing hard, cursing under his breath.

Some cops were at the window now, leaning out of it with their guns pointed downward.

"Shoot, shoot!" Boyd urged.

"Shoot who? There's two guys down there!" Kelly said.

"Shoot both—just don't let them get away!"

Kelly and the others at the window started firing.

Bullets hummed past Tracker's head, plowed up the earth at his heels. He zigzagged like a broken field runner, swiftly reversing course, darting and weaving.

The cops in the lot were eager to join the action, but the high chainlink fence checked their pursuit. They had to settle for shooting through the fence.

One of the cops at the window said, "Damn! Every time I get a bead on that sucker, he changes direction!"

"He sure can move," Kelly said.

While the cops were occupied at the window, Boyd faded back into the adjoining office. It was empty. Water from the broken cooler flowed under the partition, soaking the carpet. The floor was littered with broken glass and plaster chips.

Wasting no time, Boyd went to the desk opposite the one that Tracker had overturned. On the desktop was a holder with two stacked trays, one for incoming paperwork and one for outgoing paperwork. Both trays were filled with documents, but the one on the bottom held something else: the murder gun.

Relief surged through Boyd was he reached under the papers and felt the gun. He plucked it out and thrust it into one of his jacket pockets. It snagged when it was only halfway in. Boyd ripped the seams of the pocket as he stuffed the gun in the rest of the way.

He looked up. The others were still at the window in the other room, shooting. They hadn't seen him. But he still wasn't in the clear. Plenty of things still remained undone. He had to wrap the murder gun in his handkerchief so it looked like the gun he had taken from Jeff's dead hand. He had to get rid of Jeff's gun. His job had been made infinitely more troublesome thanks to the interfering busybody with the sunglasses. Who was that guy, anyway? A stone pro, judging by the ease with which he'd manhandled Maggard and his squad, some of the toughest cops on the force.

Boyd went into the other room. The cops had stopped shooting.

"He got away, Lieutenant. They both did," Kelly said.

"Where'd that other guy come from?" said the cop beside him.

"Never mind about that now. A fine bunch of marksmen you are! All that shooting and not one of you hits the target!"

"Don't blame us, Lieutenant. That dude in the shades was *fast*. I never saw anybody move like that. He must bc some kind of karate motherfucker or something!"

"He sure could run," Kelly agreed.

"He won't get far," Boyd said.

6.

THE KILLER'S NAME was Al Bogardus and he didn't believe in fate. Or good and evil, heaven and hell, God and the Devil. Such fantastic notions were only a scam dreamed up by the bright boys to con the suckers. He knew better. The only crime is getting caught. People are animals and the top dog rules.

Being in the courthouse reminded him of old times. He was an ex-cop himself. He used to work in the narcotics division of the Kansas City Police Department. Kansas City, Missouri, not Kansas City, Kansas. He was a rogue cop who worked both sides of the law against the middle. He wasn't gun-shy and had killed a few men in the line of duty. His first extracurricular killing was the murder of a drug-addicted prostitute who'd been stupid enough to try to blackmail him. His next victim was a sorehead dealer who had threatened to report Al for beating him and stealing his stash. Soon after that he started methodically eliminating anyone who might endanger his illicit activities.

He had an aptitude for murder. Being a cop was the perfect cover for a killer. He marketed his skills for big bucks. He worked for organized crime kingpins, drug chieftains, labor racketeers. He got to liking the work so much that he took on contracts just to keep from being bored. In thirty-five months he killed forty-seven people. Many were bystanders who just happened to be standing between him and his mark.

He quit the cops and turned free-lance hitman. He specialized mostly in corporate work. More than a few big business honchos had an occasional need for a private assassin. It was a lucrative field, and growing. He made plenty of money and did lots of traveling.

One skill in particular set him apart from most of the others in the killer pack. He was a marksman. He'd won gold medals in departmental pistol-shooting contests. Most hitmen are at best fair shots, relying on speed and surprise to close with their marks to blow their brains out. Not Al. A dead shot with a handgun, he could hit his marks from a distance.

That's why Killer Gordon had picked him for the Mountain City courthouse hit. Gordon was a shadowy figure, a contractor of wholesale murder. Gordon was the planner on this job.

Brady Sullivan was the mark. The inside men handled everything but the actual shooting. It was a sweet setup. They even supplied a fall guy. There was no shortage of pennyless victims who'd be only too glad to kill the banker. The crooked cops grabbed the first one who came along at the right time. It might have been anyone but it happened to be Jeff Purdy. He was tailor-made for the role. He'd been heard making threats against the banker, and he had a gun in his possession when he was apprehended.

He was massively dosed with a heavy tranquilizer to keep him quiet, a sedative commonly used to pacify violent mental patients. Drugged, zombie-like, he was spirited into the office behind the back of the courtroom where Al was waiting. Jeff's gun was a good one so Al decided to use it to make the hit. That would really clinch the frame. Jeff's fingerprints were all over the gun. Al wore thin latex gloves to avoid leaving any fingerprints of his own.

When it was time to move Brady out of the courthouse, Maggard tipped off Al by saying, "Here they come," the prearranged code signal. Al stood the befuddled Jeff up by the door and stuck a gun in his hand. It was the same make and model as Jeff's gun, but it was loaded with blanks.

When the banker came down the hallway, Al pushed Jeff hard out the door and opened fire. He stayed hidden behind the doorframe with only the tip of the gun sticking out. Every shot he pumped into Brady was lethal. Maggard started shooting at the same time. It all happened in the blink of an eye, too fast for any of the suckers to get wise.

Al closed the door, locked it, went into the inner office and locked the partition door. He stashed the gun under some papers in the desktop tray, went into the adjacent office and locked the connecting door. He took out his own gun, a 9mm pistol, just in case the cops tried to cross him. Such treachery was unlikely, since Killer Gordon was brokering the job, but Al wasn't a trusting sort.

The arrangement was that the inside men would run interference for him, keeping all others away from his hiding place. Boyd could do that easily because he was in charge. He'd signal Al when the coast was clear for him to make his getaway. Not even a getaway, since there wouldn't be any alarm out for him. All he had to do was walk out the door and slip away in the confusion. A piece of cake, especially with a detective lieutenant and a patrol sergeant covering for him.

That was the plan.

Al was really thrown for a loop when the melee erupted in the hall. It sounded like a kung-fu movie out there. Where did this wild free-for-all fit in the scheme of things? Al decided against sticking around to find out.

The office next door sounded like it was being demolished. Al lost his cool. He blasted some slugs through the door without thinking. He couldn't help it, he was spooked.

He grabbed the slatted window blinds in both hands and tore them off the window. He used a desk chair to smash the window, cascading crystal shards to the ground below.

Al dropped the chair and filled his hand with the gun. He clambered up on the waist-high windowsill. It was clear down below, with no cops waiting.

He jumped out the window.

He landed heavily, and his right ankle folded up on him, pitching him face down into the dirt. Even then he was careful to keep from jamming the gun muzzle into the soil.

He raised himself to his knees, bones aching. Instinct, a hunch, made him look back. He saw the stranger standing at the window, looking down at him.

The sight of him acted on Al like salt on a wound. Teeth gritted, he snapped a shot at the stranger. He knew it would miss even as he squeezed the trigger. Again, the stranger was a split-second ahead of the bullet. It wasn't natural. It was weird, uncanny.

Al's gun didn't have a silencer. Its report drew attention to him from some of the cops on the ground. They shouted, pointing at him. They were still too far off to be dangerous, but that would change fast.

Al got up and started running. Hobbling, actually. His ankle wasn't broken but it was badly sprained. It would hold up all right as long as he kept his weight off it. Working his good leg for all it was worth, dragging his stiff bad leg behind him, he scuttled toward the east side of the hill.

He was near the edge of the grounds when the cops opened up and really started shooting. They weren't shooting at him. They were shooting at the stranger who was chasing Al. Mad with frustration, Al stumbled to the hilltop's edge.

The hillside dropped away into a shallow curve the length of a football field before butting up against a street. The grassy slope was dotted with bushes and bare of all but a few skinny trees.

Footfalls pounded behind Al. The stranger had survived the gauntlet of police gunfire and was no more than fifty feet away. He still wore his sunglasses, which improbably remained in place despite his acrobatics. Beneath the sinister black visor, his chiseled face was blank, expressionless. He wasn't even breathing hard!

He kept on coming like some kind of human machine. This time Al would shut him down for good. Dropping into a combat crouch, holding his gun in a two-handed grip, Al took careful aim and fired.

He couldn't miss—but he did! All at once the stranger was a blur of motion, faking left, dodging right, weaving and reversing. His movements seemed random, arbitrary, but they always took him out of the path of the next bullet. He was still coming, and now he was much closer.

"The guy's not human!" Al said. Involuntarily he backed away. He'd forgotten how close he was to the edge. He stepped into empty air and fell backward down the hillside. He jerked the trigger as he went over, firing into the sky. He fell only a few feet before his back hit the ground, but that started him rolling. He tumbled backward down the slope.

The world was a rush of topsy-turvy motion. Stones gouged him, roots bruised him, thorns ripped him. Somehow he managed to hold on to the gun.

He thudded to a stop on a level path of ground in the middle of the hillside. He was dazed, with the wind knocked out of him.

Sirens shrieked. He heard them through the ringing in his ears. Police sirens. That cut through the fog numbing his senses. He rolled on his side, got to his knees. His index finger was still looped through the trigger guard but was bent at an unnatural angle. It was broken.

He could deal with that. He was a better shot with his left hand than most men were with their right. Switching the gun to his other hand, he accidentally twisted his finger so that the broken bones ground against a nerve. He went white with agony, but the pain helped to clear his head.

He looked up in time to see the stranger hurtling down the hillside, descending in leaps and bounds like a gazelle. Sidestepping when Al raised his gun, he ducked behind some bushes. Al couldn't see him any more. He knew the other was hiding in the bushes but a fat lot of good that did him. He couldn't even hit the stranger when he could see him.

A trumpet blast sounded somewhere nearby, an irritating one-note that set his teeth on edge as it got louder and louder. For a second, Al thought it was coming from inside his head, that it was the sound of him going nuts. The volume increased until it actually hurt his ears. The rude brassy sound was accompanied by the low bass throbbing of powerful machinery. A car horn was being held down to make that steady blast of noise. The horn of the getaway car.

Terrace Street stretched north–south, running parallel to the east side of the municipal plaza at the bottom of the hill. That's where the getaway car was waiting.

The wheelman was Denny Halftown. He came from even farther back East than Al, all the way from the Keystone State of Pennsylvania. He, too, had been recruited for the job by Killer Gordon. Denny was twenty-seven but looked ten years older. He was a weasely little speed freak who wore long sleeves year-round to hide the needle tracks on his arms from mainlining crystal meth. He had bright eyes and rotten teeth. He was fidgety and was a chain smoker of menthol-tipped cigarettes.

His specialty was driving. He was a top wheelman. He'd piloted the getaway car on big-money heists, delivered stolen autos for hot-car rings, and transported every kind of contraband from moonshine to cocaine. He'd been busted a few times but never when he was driving. He'd killed when he had to, and sometimes when he didn't have to but thought he could get away with it, but driving was his business.

Today he was driving a dark green sedan, a late-model American muscle car. It had a super-charged V–8 engine and a specially modified chassis. Its licence plates had been stolen from another car an hour before Denny and Al went out on the job.

Terrace Street was the closest Denny could get to the courthouse. That was okay with him but tough on Bogardus if he got in a jam. If all went according to plan, the hitman would exit the courthouse via a side door in the east wall, descend a stone stairway to the street below, and ride off in the waiting getaway car.

According to the planners, the deal would go down without a hitch; but then, what else were they going to say? Denny didn't sweat it too much. He was being paid to take risks. He wasn't afraid of trouble as long as it came when he was behind the wheel.

He'd visited the site the day before to get the lay of the land. He'd examined the main roads, intersections, side streets. He'd mapped out a number of alternate routes for the getaway.

Gordon's people on the scene had provided the wheels, hardware, accommodations, and support services.

Earlier today Denny had taken his position, parking under the overhanging branches of some evergreen trees on Terrace Street. He parked facing north on the two-way street and waited.

If there's one thing a wheelman hates, it's having to turn off the car's engine, even for a moment. There's always that chance, however slim, of the car not starting again due to some mechanical fluke. Denny switched off his car, hating it. It was necessary. He might be waiting some length of time, and he didn't want to attract the attention of some ecology-minded busybody by running the motor while the car was standing. He didn't want to be noticed by anyone who later might be fingering him in a police line-up.

The mid-morning sun was hot, but the shade from the trees kept the car interior cooled. Denny sat in the driver's seat with the window rolled down. A baseball cap was pulled down low over his eyes and a local newspaper folded to the sports section was propped up on the steering wheel. That's all it was, a prop, to make him look like Joe Citizen.

The municipal plaza was on the top of a ridge. Terrace Street was the first street below it on the eastern slope. Other streets lower down were wider and more accessible, so they were more often used by the public. The morning traffic on Terrace Street was light to moderate, mostly light.

Police cars cruised by at the rate of about one every fifteen minutes or so. They weren't interested in Denny; they had bigger fish to fry. They couldn't spare a second glance at a citizen sitting peacefully in his car in a legal parking zone.

Fastened under the dashboard was an all-frequency radio receiver tuned to the police wave bands. Mountain City and state police used two different frequencies. The set was pre-tuned to both wavelengths, one of the benefits of having an inside man in the cops. Denny switched back and forth between the two settings.

As an added precaution, the receiver was hidden inside a phony housing that made it look like a stereo tape player. Attention to detail—that was Killer Gordon for you.

Denny had arrived early, before the morning session had even been called to order. There was no way of knowing in advance when the hearing would be adjourned. It might happen shortly after the lawyers made their opening arguments, or it might drag on all the way to the noon recess. Whenever it ended, they'd be hustling the defendant out of the courthouse shortly thereafter.

That's when the hit would go down.

Until then, there was nothing for Denny to do but wait and monitor the police radio net. That alerted him to the hearing's end. The radio traffic suddenly multiplied as the tactical unit commanders broadcast instructions to the troops to head off chaos.

A van moved north on Terrace Street. It moved slowly, at less than ten miles per hour. Denny watched its approach in his rear-view mirror.

Rumbling, it drew up alongside him. A medium-sized brown van with a curved tinted windshield and dark side windows that screened off the inside of the cab from his view. All he could see of the driver and his passenger were shadowy blurs. The van's solid body was windowless. There was a clear plastic bubble set in the middle of the roof.

The vehicle bristled with a half-dozen different varieties of antennas. A pair of long vertical ones rose like metal buggy whips from the rear bumper. Others were shaped like miniature TV antennas, coiled into funnels, or were round and spiky like steel sea urchins. Additionally, a gimbal-mounted device resembling nothing so much as a satellite receiving dish a foot in diameter was set at each of the four corners of the van's roof.

Maintaining its steady pace, the van passed Denny. Its well-tuned engine hummed with power under restraint. It was heavier than it looked and rode fairly low on its tires. The exhaust system had been customized to suppress engine noise.

It turned left at the next intersection, going west on Farview Road, passing the courthouse parking lot driveway as it climbed to the top of the ridge.

Probably a TV news wagon, Denny thought. That would explain all the antennas and why the vehicle rode so low. It must be loaded inside with heavy communications hardware. Funny, though, that it was bare of any logo identifying its parent station. Maybe it kept a low profile to avoid attracting attention.

The van moved out of sight, and he stopped thinking about it.

He didn't need a police band radio to tell him when the riot started. He could hear the uproar from where he was sitting. He couldn't see it, he was too far north, but he could hear it.

The hit would be going down any minute now. He started the car. The engine turned over on the first try. The car quivered with powerful vibrations.

He was trembling all over, not with fear but with eagerness to leave the starting gate. Energized by a rush of adrenaline.

The shooting turned the police radio traffic into a stew of shouted babel. No one knew what was happening and everyone was trying to find out at once.

He stuck his head out the open window, craning for a view. A flash of motion caught his eye. A woman was standing at the top of the stone stairway connecting Courthouse Hill with Terrace Street. She wasn't a policewoman, at least not a uniformed one. She wore a business suit and skirt.

That complicated things. According to plan, Al Bogardus was supposed to be coming down those steps. Too bad for the woman if she got a good look at his face. He wasn't likely to leave her alive if she did.

As it turned out, Al didn't descend by the stairs. Denny

glimpsed him standing outlined at the edge of the hill a few hundred feet north of the stairway. His gun was blasting away.

Denny watched in amazement as Al stepped backward off the hill and tumbled downward head over heels. For a moment he thought that Al had been shot.

A figure suddenly leaped into view, hurling himself feet-first off the hillcrest. He touched ground thirty feet below, then bounced sideways for another ten feet, an unexpected change in direction that not so coincidentally landed him behind the cover of a large rock. His form dwindled behind the rock so that Denny couldn't see him at all.

Denny blinked.

In the next instant, the figure reappeared, jumping down the incline at a different angle. Flitting shadowlike across the ground, he leapfrogged and zigzagged downhill in pursuit of Al.

Al rose shakily to his feet and reeled trying to stay on them.

That clinched it. Al was alive. Denny couldn't bug out and leave him behind. If he did and Al should by some chance escape, the hitman wouldn't rest until he had Denny's guts for breakfast.

Denny stomped the gas pedal, threw the car into gear. Wheels whirled, smoking. Tires took hold and the car leaped forward.

Denny drove across the street at a diagonal. There were two quick bumps as the front and back wheels went over the curb. The car crossed the sidewalk and tore across the lower slope. Denny pointed the car at Al, driving straight for him. It barreled up the hill, trailing a wake of twigs, dirt, and dead leaves.

Al swayed unsteadily on his feet, as if he were drunk. *Punchy*, Denny thought. He pounded the horn with the heel of his hand, beating out an urgent fanfare. Al didn't seem to notice it.

The angle of incline increased as Denny neared the middle slope. Gravity pressed him back into his seat. He held down the horn so that it sounded in one ear-shattering blast.

Denny turned the car to the right so it ran parallel with the ridge. He worked the brakes carefully to keep from sliding. Even so the car slid for the last two dozen feet or so across the grass before lurching to a halt in Al's vicinity.

Cops appeared at the top of the hill and started shooting. They didn't hit anything.

Al broke and ran toward the car. He didn't bother with the

door, he just dove headfirst through the open rear window. The car was in motion before Al hit the floor.

Even as Denny was thinking that the cops didn't have the range, one of them shot out his sideview mirror. "Seven years bad luck for you, cop!" Denny said.

A blur flashed at him from the side. It was the acrobat, the guy who'd been chasing Al. He was uphill of the car and raced downward toward it at an angle, trying to head it off. He'd never reach it in time. So Denny thought, until the stranger suddenly launched himself into space. There was a tremendous impact as he came crashing down on the roof.

"Damn!" Denny shouted.

Al had fallen between the front seat and the back seat. He rolled over and fired into the roof, blasting holes into it.

The din of gunfire hammered at Denny's eardrums, partially deafening him. He whipped the steering wheel to the nine o'clock position, then three o'clock, then twelve o'clock. The car fishtailed in response. The maneuver dislodged the stranger from the roof, or maybe Al had hit him.

The car handled differently when relieved of the stranger's weight. Denny pointed the nose downward and descended the slope at an angle. It was a rough rumbling ride, but he knew the specially modified suspension and reinforced tires could take it. The car bounced, jounced, and shook, scraping its underside into the dirt.

Al peered out the rear window. "Still alive—?" Al said, gasping. Without warning he smashed the gun butt against the rear window.

The window chipped. Al slammed it with the gun butt again. This time the glass cratered. Spiderweb cracks haloed the point of impact. Really pissed off, Al hit it a third time. The safety glass frosted and shattered.

"The fuck are you doing?"

Al stuck his gun out of the hole where the window used to be and started shooting. "Now I got him!" He fired off the rest of the clip, emptying it.

"Fuck! I missed him!"

"Who is that guy?" Denny shouted back over his shoulder.

"A devil!"

The car took the curb with a bump and bottomed out into the street, its underside striking sparks against the pavement. Al bounced and hit his head against the roof. He tumbled into the well between the seats.

Denny jockeyed the wheel with some fancy handling. The engine roared with high RPMs. Wheels bit, squealed. The car took off, heading north on Terrace.

Sirens whoop-wailed, dopplering closer. A police car dropped down Farview Road.

Collision was imminent. The police car hit the brakes. The nose dipped, the wheels locked, the car skidded.

Denny clipped the police car, sideswiping its right front fender with his car's reinforced steel bumper. There was the sound of grinding metal and breaking glass.

Denny knew what he was doing. He hit the other car at just the right angle to crush its fender against the wheel, immobilizing it. He stepped harder on the gas as he turned the steering wheel the other way, tearing free. The nerve-racking shriek of metal against metal suddenly ended as the getaway car broke loose.

"Crazy bastard!" Al said. "I ought to blow your head off!"

"He ain't chasing us, is he?"

Al looked back. Sure enough, the police car was disabled. The front side was pushed in, the crumpled hood had popped open. The crash cracked the radiator; steam poured out of the engine compartment. The car slanted sideways across the street, blocking other police cars from taking up the chase.

"Fasten your seatbelt, we're gonna be doing some driving," Denny said.

The straightaway was wide open. Denny stood on the gas.

7.

Tracker was a master of high-speed combat. As a fighter jet ace, he'd prevailed in supersonic dogfights, where the outcome was decided in the first few seconds of the engagement. As a martial artist, the proud holder of the coveted third-degree black belt in the Sun Moo Kwan style of Tae Kwon Do, he'd spent hundreds of hours of free-style sparring with formidable opponents in the dojo to sharpen his skills.

That's how he was able to dodge Al's bullets. Al was a good shot, but every nuance of his body language betrayed his next move in advance to Tracker. His stance and form determined where he would shoot. Tracker waited each time until Al was totally committed to an action before responding to it. In effect, this meant waiting until Al's finger was tightening on the trigger before dodging out of the line of fire.

When Al was on the verge of shooting, his eyes narrowed, veins throbbed in his forehead, and his jaws flexed. These were involuntarily muscular reactions of which he was not aware. But the magnifying power of Tracker's zoom lens eyes brought Al's telltale ticks and twitches into sharp focus.

There was a tingling behind the backs of Tracker's eyes. The computerized electro-optics were being asked to do too much. Subvocally he cut the Input recording function out of real time. Instead of operating non-stop, the system now sampled the data flow crossing Tracker's video-sonic sensors in periodic intervals.

Tracker immediately benefitted from the lower power drain. The tingling lessened, but did not vanish altogether.

Tracker's ultrasonic echo-locator detected motion behind and to one side of him.

A woman was descending the stone stairway with skirt fluttering and long legs flashing. She held one hand cupped up close to her mouth and seemed to speak into it.

Tracker zoomed in for a close-up. It was Anne, the woman he'd encountered briefly in front of the courthouse. She was talking into some kind of hand-held radio. He couldn't spare the time to scan the wavelength band for the frequency on which she was broadcasting.

Anne was not openly armed. A weapon might have been hidden in her handbag.

Tracker acquired her, tagging her image for future identification, registering it as a potential target with the ATR/Search program.

She was alone. Where was her companion, the belligerent Branton?

The getaway car plowed into Terrace Street and catapulted northward.

Anne descended to the bottom of the stairs. A silver-black Mercedes pulled up to the curb alongside her, pointing northward on the wrong side of the street. Branton was the driver.

A car. Tracker needed a car to continue the chase and to escape from the cops who were chasing him. Chase, hell; they were shooting to kill but their aim wasn't too good.

Tracker tagged Branton and his car. He did it as he rushed toward the car. Toward Anne and Branton. Maybe the cops wouldn't be so quick to shoot for fear of hitting them.

Tracker's easy loping strides were deceptively quick. He closed the distance with such speed that he was upon Anne Bellamy and Branton almost before they knew it. Anne froze, standing near the car. Branton scowled.

Tracker moved to the driver's side. The window was open. Branton stuck his face out at Tracker, saying, "What do you want?"

"May I borrow your car, please?"

"What is this, a joke?"

"No."

"Go to hell!"

"I insist," Tracker said.

Branton's hand plunged inside his jacket, clawing for a gun. Tracker's fist shot out in a short hard jab that landed right on the button. There was a sharp popping sound as his knuckles impacted Branton's jaw.

Branton stiffened. His eyes rolled up in his head so that only the whites showed. He fell forward, unconscious.

Tracker caught Branton's head before it smashed face-first into the steering wheel. He opened the door and hauled out Branton's limp form, stretching him out on the curbside verge.

Anne unfastened the catch of her pocketbook and reached inside.

"Uh-uh," Tracker said.

Maybe she could have reached her weapon and brought it into play before he reached her; maybe not. For whatever reason, she held her hand.

"Better take cover. The local law isn't too particular about who it shoots," Tracker said.

She was cool, unsmiling, intent.

Tracker reached under Branton's coat and lifted his gun. It was a big .357, chrome-plated with a mirror finish. Despite the glitz it was a big-bore gun with plenty of man-stopping power. A man-killer.

"Tell your friend I said thanks for the loan," Tracker said, sliding behind the wheel of the car.

"Careful," she said. "You might catch what you're chasing."

"I hope so," he said, pointedly looking her up and down.

"I didn't mean me," Anne said.

"You must like me if you're worried about me."

"I want you to live long enough to appreciate the full extent of your ignorance."

"Nice," Tracker said. "I get the last word, though."

He floored the gas pedal, speed-shifting through the gears as the high-powered Mercedes took off like a rocket.

Some cops opened fire as Tracker whipped past them. A shot blew out both of the rear side windows, another pulverized a taillight. Then the car was out of range.

The getaway car had a good lead, but Tracker was hot on the trail. The Mercedes was a high-performance machine capable of maintaining the pace. And Tracker's zoom lenses could keep the other car in sight long after it would have been lost to normal vision.

His optic nerves were still tingling. He halved the Input Sampler rate, enjoying instant relief.

The street stretched out straight ahead for some distance. On the left were rows of houses rising in steps to the top of the ridge. On the right was a vacant strip of land about fifty yards wide. Widely scattered stone foundations marked sites once occupied by houses. Now they were weedy lots.

Beyond the edge of the strip there was empty air, where the ridge ended with an abrupt drop.

Steep narrow roads branched off from the left side of the street, connecting it with the top of the ridge. Most of them could barely accommodate one vehicle at a time and were little more than lanes. As the getaway car shot past one of these roads, a van hurtled out of it, whipped around the corner, and took off after it in hot pursuit.

Tracker zoomed in on the van, tagging it. His scientist's eye was struck by the intricate array of equipment on the van. The glittering coils and cables, the complex mechanisms whose shapes were tantalizingly half-familiar, half-strange.

Whatever it was, the van was no TV news wagon. Tracker knew that at first glance. The external hardware had nothing to do with broadcasting or receiving television signals. It was designed to handle a staggering amount of power. Look at the size of those insulators! *If* they were insulators. And those cables were as thick as rattlesnakes!

This was important. Tracker boosted the Input into full real-time recording capacity for complete coverage. The tingling returned in full force. An itch, maddeningly unscratchable, made itself felt behind his eyes. He was now significantly closer to overload. A margin of safety still remained, but it was much narrower. He should switch off Input, but how could he, when each passing second brought new marvels?

Something was happening. The van's image began to flash and flicker. It sparkled and shimmered with bands of diamond-colored energy. A shining aura outlined the van, all but the wheels. Of course! The tires were made of nonconductive rubber

From far behind came the wail of police sirens. The van was no police vehicle but it was chasing the getaway car. Why? Was it part of some mysterious third force working at cross-purposes to the killer and those who had hired him?

Whatever it was, the van was equipped with some advanced technology. The energy patterns enveloping it were complex and subtle. They would have been invisible to the naked eye. Even Tracker's video eyes had trouble receiving the energy field.

A hatch opened under the clear plastic bubble on top of the van. An instrument rose from below, filling the bubble. It was a curious device, a boxy metal trapezoid with a cone-shaped funnel at one end.

A section of the bubble dome slid open, the section which had been in front of the device's funnel. The funnel was pointing toward the getaway car up ahead. Sparks as big as dinner plates started to snap on the bubble dome and on the antennas arrayed behind it. The field outlining the van brightened to a blue glow visible to ordinary human vision.

The power supply had been dramatically increased.

Denny drove. Al reloaded his 9mm. He said, "What I need is a fucking machine-gun!"

Denny didn't hear him. He was in sync with his machine. He felt every bump and pebble as the car skimmed across the surface of the road.

Al watched the van moving up from behind. It was still a good distance away but it was moving fast.

"Where'd that bastard come from?" Al said.

Denny, intent, did not reply.

"What am I doing, fucking talking to myself here or what?" Al said.

"Don't distract me, man. I'm driving."

"Well, drive then! Step on it and lose this guy!"

"I *am* stepping on it!" It was true. Al could hear the engine winding higher and higher as Denny bore down on the gas. But they weren't pulling away from the van; in fact they could barely maintain their lead. "That ain't cops!" Denny said. "Cops ain't got no wheels that fast!"

Denny, tightlipped, pushed the pedal closer to the floor. A moment later, he said, "What kind of mill they got in that damn thing?"

"You lousy no-driving son of a bitch," Al fumed. "All right.

All right. If you can't shake 'em, let 'em catch up. I'll take care of the bastards my way, 9mm style!"

Denny eased up slightly on the accelerator. The van immediately surged forward, narrowing the gap.

"C'mon, pally, a little closer," Al urged the van.

Sunlight bounced off the van's curved windshield, turning it semiopaque. Al, squinting, saw two shadowy forms in the operator's cab.

The semiauto pistol spat out slugs as fast as Al could pull the trigger. The bullets flattened against the windshield and ricocheted screaming off into space. The windshield was bulletproof. "Bulletproof" glass will shatter if shot enough times in the same place. So Al believed, and he wasted no time in acting on that theory. He fed a fresh clip into his gun. Snarling, defiant, exultant, he resumed firing.

The van counterattacked. Its body was hard and shiny, like a brown beetle. It began to glint and flash until it was spiky with daggers of light. It sparkled so brightly that it hurt Al's eyes. He stopped shooting.

The getaway car and the van were bunched up close together, Tracker's Mercedes was farther behind them, and the police pursuit was far to the rear.

A blue glow outlined the van. Blue foxfire crackled on the antenna array, the clear bubble dome, and the strange projecting device that rose into view on the roof. Al wasn't fooled by the gizmo's resemblance to a motion picture projector. He knew a weapon when he saw one. The gizmo's wide funnel looked too much like a big-bore gun barrel. His worst suspicions were confirmed when the swivel-mounted device turned a few degrees clockwise to bring the funnel straight in line with his car.

Al raised his gun to shoot the glittering gizmo. A blue disk winked on inside the funnel, startling him so that he held his fire. The disk blazed bright blue.

The getaway car started experiencing engine troubles. The motor sputtered, shuddered, and started missing.

Denny thought he was going to have a heart attack. He felt like he'd been frozen solid in a block of ice, so great was his terror at the inexplicable malfunction. He'd painstakingly checked out this car himself in preparation for the run, as he always did before a job. It was a cream puff, one sweet honey of a piece of machinery. Its high-performance engine couldn't possibly be breaking down. But it was. The motor lost power and the steering became balky. Denny had to fight for control of the wheel.

The police band radio was going nuts, too, emitting a torrent of white noise and howling feedback.

The car's performance worsened as the gizmo's blue disk shone ever brighter. The disk blazed brighter than the sun. Al couldn't look at it directly, the glare was too painful. He held his hand over his eyes, shielding them, trying to get the gizmo lined up in his sights to blast it.

It blasted first.

The shining disc ballooned into a sphere of crackling energy, a ball of blue fire. Leaping free of the funnel, it launched itself at the getaway car.

The engine had almost quit, but forward momentum kept the car going at a high rate of speed. The fireball was faster and overtook it in a few seconds. The fireball seemed to rush straight toward Al, who was cowering in the back seat, his gun forgotten. Harsh blue light filled the car.

Denny screamed, the steering wheel dead in his hands.

The fireball wasn't made of the flames of burning. It was made of electric fire, raw force, a highly unstable bundle of high energy. It was so close that Al could almost touch it. His skin tingled and his hair stood on end. He covered his eyes. The blue light was so bright that he could see the bones of his hand, like an X-ray.

The fireball touched the car.

The gates of Hell opened up.

The last thought of Al Bogardus, not a superstitious man, was that the Devil had reached out for him to claim his own.

8.

TRACKER HOPED HIS electro-optical system would keep from overloading long enough for him to see the end result of the van's unknown energizing process. Overload was near. The demand on the opti-visor's micro-circuitry was spiking the power curves toward the critical redline.

He was crowding the safety limits of the apparatus. He felt as if cigar butts were being stubbed out in the pits of his eyes. The heat was a byproduct of the heavy work being done by the electro-optics. The pain was intense but not physically destructive. The system would shut down before the threshold of organic damage was reached.

fIn the meantime, it was vital that he input as much coverage of the van as he could get. He'd need it later for reconstruction and analysis of the tremendous forces being harnessed by the mystery vehicle.

The van's energizing process began affecting Tracker's car. The motor started to run rough as its sparkplugs misfired. The steering became clumsy, unresponsive. Tracker guessed that the energizing somehow interfered with nearby power sources, such as the auto's electrical system. He wasn't as close to the van as the getaway car was, so the Mercedes was less influenced by it.

At least he didn't have to worry about the force field affecting his electro-optics. He'd designed the system so it would be impervious to external EMG fluctuations. That was a basic and utterly necessary precaution for a man whose work on the cutting edge of the techno-frontier routinely took him to physics labs, particle accelerators, radar stations, atomic power plants, and other installations whose standard measuring unit was the MEV, the million electron-volt. No, his electro-optics were hardened against outside interference.

The van hurtled forward without slackening. Its automotive system must have been insulated against interference from the force field. The blue glow outlining it indicated that some form of ionization was taking place, although that could have been a side-effect of the energization rather than its real purpose.

Machinery hidden inside the van generated the power, the antenna array channeled it, and the bubble dome projecting device was the force's delivery system. The mechanized projector lined its funnel up with the getaway car like a compass needle zeroing in on magnetic north. A blue globe bubbled out of the funnel's wide muzzle, clinging to its lip. A ball of pure energy, it blazed so brightly that its seething core whited out on Tracker's view screen. Detaching itself from the launcher, the fireball sped through space in pursuit of the getaway car.

Fireball? Hardly. Tracker knew it for what it was, a high-energy plasmatic sphere. Ball lightning, to put it simply. The raw power of a thunderbolt concentrated in spherical form.

Manmade lightning.

Harnessing the power of the electron was an awesome achievement in itself, but there was more. The lightning ball was directional. It took off after the getaway car like a homing pigeon. The blue glow outlining the van disappeared at the instant the lightning ball separated from the launcher. The blue globe swiftly overtook the car. At the last instant it swooped down and flew up the tailpipe.

The car blew up.

Tracker could guess what had happened. The lightning ball was highly unstable. When it touched its target it came undone, discharging its considerable energy all in one great blast. The lightning ball burst with a blinding flash—literally blinding, as far as Tracker was concerned. His video eyes were protected by a number of built-in safety features. The added strain of trying to cope with the too-bright light kicked the system into overload.

The world went dark. Tracker was smothered in blackness as

intense and unrelieved as that of a sunless cave buried a mile below the earth's crust. The system had shut down, blacking out. Tracker was blind at the wheel of a speeding car—

—Sight returned.

All at once, Tracker could see again. His view screen had switched back on almost immediately after blacking out, but the few seconds of sightlessness had seemed like an eternity to Tracker.

The getaway car jetted a fiery pillar a hundred feet straight up into the air. Real fire, not electro-plasmic energy. The gas tank had exploded as if struck by lightning, which in a sense it had been. All the gas in the tank had spontaneously combusted in an incendiary blast.

The car—with Al and Denny in it—was instantly consumed by fire. The explosion flipped the car. The fast-moving funeral pyre skidded for a few dozen yards before hitting the curb. The impact set it rolling. It rolled for a hundred feet before stopping, a red-hot heap of fused, scorched metal.

There was no more left of Al and Denny than there would be of two moths who had flown into a bonfire. A strip of burning grass and weeds a hundred feet long marked the path to the cremated car's stopping place. The van passed it without slowing.

Jeff Purdy's killer was dead, along with his wheelman accomplice. Hellfire itself could not have incinerated them any more thoroughly. But they were only hirelings, specialists hired to do a job. Behind them there was a contractor, and beyond that a conspiracy, one involving looted banks and lost millions and crooked cops.

It would have to wait. Tracker had a new objective, one that took precedence over hunting down the masterminds behind Jeff's murder. Mountain City's ills were a strictly local affair in comparison to the overriding national security importance of the lightning ball.

The van was his objective now. Van? It was an EMG war wagon. Directed Energy, the long-sought goal of the advanced weapons experimenters, harder to find than the Holy Grail. The best brains of the nation's most secret R & D defense labs were nowhere near unlocking the secret of DEWs—Directed Energy Weapons. DEWs, the heat ray and zap gun of science fiction fame.

The technology already existed to make weapons that would have been right at home in the futuristic world of Buck Rogers. The laser is a heat ray. Particle beam accelerators shoot beams of protons, neutrons, electrons. But the hardware was at a relatively crude level of early development. Primitive. Size was a limiting factor. Scientists could build a billion-dollar atom-smasher, but they were a long way off from a practical application of their theories in the form of a lightweight, portable energy weapon that could be mass-produced for a sum less than the national debt.

Until a few minutes ago, Tracker had thought he knew as much about the state of most secret energy weapons research as anyone in the field. Now, he knew he was wrong.

Whoever had chained the lightning knew more. And Tracker thought he knew the inventor's real identity.

The genius that chained the thunderbolt could change the balance of world power. The lightning ball was a quantum jump ahead of the current generation of DEWs. The nation that first mastered the technology would have a formidable strategic advantage over all the others. And yet this revolutionary breakthrough in destructive weaponry had been unleashed in Mountain City in broad daylight to annihilate a mob-style hitman and his getaway driver. Talk about overkill! It was like burning down a building to get rid of a few rats. The lightning lord must be supremely arrogant to so openly stage a demonstration of his power. Arrogant to the point of madness.

Arrogant? Or supremely confident?

Vacant lots and patches of woods lined both sides of the street on the ridge north of Courthouse Hill. There were few houses and less traffic and no pedestrians. It was a small miracle that no oncoming vehicle had blundered into the path of the chase yet.

The pursuing police cars weren't as far back as they had been, but they hadn't been close enough to see the lightning ball. They'd seen the getaway car burst into a pillar of flame, but they'd think the blast had been caused by a conventional weapon, like a bomb planted in the car or a bullet detonating the fuel tank.

Suddenly the bubble dome rotated in one direction and the projector spun in the opposite direction. When they both stopped moving, the firing port in the dome was aligned with the bore of the launching tube, which was aimed at Tracker.

The van re-energized, enveloped in a crackling blue aura. It powered up much faster than it had the first time. Reached full power within ten seconds.

The Mercedes sputtered, slowed.

The cop cars neared.

A blazing energy globe formed on the muzzle of the projector.

Blue light shone through the windshield, flooding the car. Light so bright that it cast hard-edged shadows. The shadows were midnight blue, not black.

Even with all its resources on call, the opti-visor was hard-pressed to stabilize the blue globe's incandescent image on the view screen. It shivered on the verge of white-out, where too much light registers as pure white brilliancy on the screens.

Blue-white lightnings radiated from the edge of the blue globe like the tentacles of a jellyfish, swirling, curling, and rippling. Electro-flagella, possibly a vital clue as to how the energy structure was stabilized as ball lightning.

Tracker ached to input the valuable data, but he didn't dare. A few seconds of overload-induced temporary blindness had given him a renewed respect for the tolerance loads of the E-OP system. Besides, the question was academic. He had run out of time to study the phenomenon as a detached observer. He was now an active participant in a potentially fatal field test. The blue globe had been fired. At him.

Gears grinding, tires squealing, the car swerved hard to the right to avoid the onrushing fireball. The fireball changed course to intercept it.

The Mercedes hopped the curb at an angle, its left front fender grazing a tree trunk as the car left the road. It plowed diagonally across a weedy lot, its wheels gouging two broad furrows. It had slowed but was still moving fast enough for Tracker to break his neck if he bailed out too soon.

The far edge of the lot neared and beyond it loomed empty space. The lightning ball would overtake Tracker before his car sailed off the edge. It was less than two car lengths behind him and closing fast.

Tracker called on an old trick, a risky evasive maneuver known as the "bootlegger's turn" after its inventors. He threw on the emergency brake and whipped the steering wheel as far to the right as it would go. The brakes caught, the wheels gripped, and the car started spinning. It was still skidding out of control toward the edge of a cliff, but at a much slower rate. Spinning like a top ate up much of its forward momentum.

The ploy bought Tracker a few extra seconds of life by causing the fast-flying blue globe to overshoot its mark. It outraced the spinning car, soaring past land's end into the sky.

Tracker fought to keep all four wheels on the ground while the Mercedes whirled like a merry-go-round. Each 360-degree turn diminished his speed, but the cliff edge was only a few lengths away and rushing closer. Tracker kept his bearings as the world turned in circles. It was tame stuff compared to the aerobatic gyrations he'd endured in jet fighter combat.

The lightning ball wasn't so easily eluded. Slowing in midair, it curved its path 180-degrees, reversing direction. Its velocity had dropped to a few miles per hour at the top of the curve, as if it had lost the scent and was trying to find it. Once it reversed course and started retracing its route, it gathered speed, accelerating toward the car.

Tracker popped open the catch of the seat belt, shouldered open the door, and threw himself clear of the pinwheeling car. He hit the ground rolling and kept on rolling. The firestorm could kill him as dead as the thunderbolt if he was too near the car when it blew.

The car came to a stop a little less than six feet away from the precipice, turned so that its front was pointed at the street.

The blue globe swooped down, merging with it in a mad ecstatic rush.

What resulted was three blasts in one.

The first blast was caused by the lightning ball's discorporation, loosing the tremendous fury of its unchained energies. Auto glass and metal melted like ice under a blowtorch. Tires liquefied. The second blast was caused by the raw electricity detonating the car's fuel tank. A roiling orange-red fireball engulfed the car, then thrust upward into the sky, a fiery spear. The third blast was a sonic one, a thunderclap that followed the lightning ball as it would have followed a natural lightning bolt.

The three blasts came in such quick succession that they seemed to be one titanic explosion.

The concussion hammered sky and earth. Shockwaves picked up Tracker and threw him toward the edge of the cliff.

He'd been at the edge of the blast zone and had taken a pounding that left his senses stunned. He was flying through the air. Heat waves from the burning car crashed against him. He was careful not to breathe, for fear of scorching his lungs with superheated air. He spread-eagled his limbs to maximize air resistance and slow his headlong flight.

A patch of thornbushes barred the way. Tracker crossed his arms in front of his face to protect it. Spiky thorns tore at his body, scourging him. His garments offered some protection. He tore at the vines and tendrils, snatching for a handhold. Each time he got one, the thing he was grabbing broke. He used his feet, too, trying to hook them around stems and branches. The thornbushes were a barbed net trying to snare him. Ahead, empty air loomed in all directions.

A sapling rushed toward him at an angle. He hooked his right arm around it, catching its slender trunk in the crook of his elbow. The sapling flattened on the ground. Tracker got both hands around it, clutching the rope-thin shaft with a double-vise grip. His grip held but the sapling didn't. It started to tear loose from the ground. Tracker dug his heels into the earth, fighting for traction. Suddenly there was no more ground, and his feet were thrashing empty air.

There was a sharp sudden snapping pull that he felt deep in the sockets of his arms. The sapling had refused to be torn free and had stayed stubbornly rooted in the earth. It was Tracker's lifeline. It had stopped him at the very brink of the cliff. He'd been about to go over the edge feet-first. From the knees down, his legs were sticking out in the void. He squirmed all the way back to solid ground. The thorns had scratched him up pretty good.

The smell of ozone was thick in the air, overpowering even the stinks of puddled rubber, hot metal, oil, and burning gasoline. The ozone left an exhilarating freshness like that which follows an electrical storm.

The car was a half-molten slagheap sizzling in the bottom of a shallow smoking crater. A dozen or more small fires blazed near the blast area, ignited by flaming gasoline.

Tracker's hearing was impaired. Temporary partial deafness caused by the blast. It would soon pass—he hoped. If it didn't, there were ways to get around it, but he couldn't deal with that now. His electro-optic system was unhurt and continued to operate at peak efficiency. It was combat-tough, built to exacting battlefield specifications. The tough polycarbonate opti-visor could withstand explosive shockwaves that would turn flesh and blood into jelly.

Tracker scanned the scene. The van was nowhere in sight. Had it made its getaway? Certainly it had escaped him—for now. He'd lost the trail but the blue globe had failed to kill him. His first engagement with the forces of the lightning lord had ended in a draw.

The flaming wreck was a beacon for police cars. Five of them rolled up, angling nose-in at the curb opposite the blast site. Three patrol cars and two unmarked cars. The patrol car's emergency lights flashed like a carnival come-on, adding an oddly festive touch to the blasted landscape.

Car doors were flung open and cops poured out of them. Mountain City cops and nothing but, without a state trooper in sight. The patrol cars disgorged uniformed cops. Plainclothes detectives dismounted from the unmarked cars. Patrolmen and detectives alike were armed with big-bore handguns and shotguns. Tracker didn't see any rifles among them. That was a break.

A train whistle sounded in the distance.

The cops formed up in a long loose line facing the blast site. Lt. Boyd was in charge of the operation with Monty clinging to his heels. The cops were grim, wary, intent. They didn't look like they thought that no one had survived the car wreck. They were waiting for Tracker to show himself so they could shoot him. Of that he was certain. Boyd wouldn't rest while Tracker still lived. The sudden deaths of the hitman and his driver, and the complete and total obliteration of their bodies, the getaway car, and all the physical evidence it contained, must have seemed like a gift from the gods to Boyd.

Now only Tracker could finger him as the inside man for a cunning murder plot. Therefore Tracker must die, and quickly, before he could tell his tale where it might be believed.

The police lieutenant circulated among his men, issuing last-minute instructions to them. Probably reminding them to shoot to kill, Tracker thought sourly. The cops seemed ready to move out but they were staying put, at least for the moment. Why? Maybe they thought Tracker had a gun. He wished he did.

Branton's chrome-plated .357 had been lost when Tracker bailed out of the Mercedes.

The train whistle sounded again, closer this time.

A sixth patrol car arrived at the scene. In it were three men, two uniformed cops and a civilian. One of the cops was the driver. The other was a specialist. He toted a rifle-shaped object in a leather carrying case. The civilian was a specialist, too. He wore a neon orange baseball cap, T-shirt, jeans. Cradled in his arms was a high-powered scoped rifle, no carrying case.

The specialists were marksmen, sharpshooters. Now that they were here, the hunt could begin. The others would beat the bushes, flushing out the prey so the riflemen could down it. The hunt was delayed while the police marksman uncased his rifle and adjusted its sights. Boyd, impatient, stood breathing down the back of the rifleman's neck.

Tracker had been thrown a good distance from the wrecked car in its crater. The thornbushes gave him some cover. Wreaths and streamers of oily black smoke drifted across the ground, helping to hide him. Those hunting him couldn't see through the smoke screen, but he could.

His options were limited. He low-crawled to the edge of the cliff, looked down. The cliffs were part of the ridge north of Courthouse Hill. Mountain City's northside was mostly undeveloped country. Here, where Tracker was cornered, a more or less vertical rock wall fell two hundred feet to a railroad cut with two sets of tracks. A long freight train was making the grade on the northbound rails. Its whistle tooted shrilly.

What would have been an impassable barrier to a flatlander was an inviting stairway to an experienced mountaineer. Tracker was one. He'd been born and bred in the Colorado Rockies, scaling peaks in boyhood days which would deter veteran mountain climbers. In later years, he'd tackled some of the most challenging and dangerous climbs in the world, from the Alps to the Himalayas. Of course, those later ascents had been made with the benefit of the most advanced and effective mountaineering equipment, including crampons, pitons, safety lines, grappling hooks, and the like.

This time he was going strictly no-frills.

No shoes, either. He took off his hiking boots and socks. He stuffed his socks inside the boots and tied the boots together by their laces. He looped them around the back of his neck, wearing them like a yoke. He'd need them later, and besides, he wasn't leaving behind any physical evidence. A suspect's boot is as good as a signed confession to a skilled forensic investigator.

Shouts came from the cops. Not shouts of alarm, but instructions, marching orders. They were on the move. The line of hunters started forward, crossing the field.

Tracker lowered himself down over the edge of the cliff. He hung there by his hands, his bare feet groping for a toehold. The soles looked as hard as rock. A thin layer of calluses covered the bottoms of both feet, the result of rigorous Tae Kwon Do conditioning to transform them into deadly weapons.

Winds buffeted him, seeking to tear him loose from his precarious perch at the top of the rock wall. If he fell he'd break like an egg on the boulders at the bottom of the cliff.

He started down. Iron fingers crept into cracks in the rock, seeking handholds, testing them before the climber dared trust his weight to them. His front was flattened against stone, hugging the cliff wall. Knobs and outcroppings served as welcome stepping stones.

The rock face was splintered, jagged, irregular. It was dotted with plants and bushes sprouting almost vertically from the side of the cliff. Tracker steered clear of them. Useless at best, they could be dangerous obstacles to his descent. He concentrated on the climb. Inattention could be fatal. He mustn't divide his attention by listening for the hunters, or wondering when one of them would stick his head over the edge of the cliff for a look-see, or fretting about what a soft target he was, clinging to the rocks like a human fly.

He was a little more than halfway down the cliff when the cops spotted him. A burning mound of damp dead leaves and weeds laid down thick clouds of smoke at the summit. The smoke screen had bought him some time but it was too good to last. A rift in the smoke let a cop see Tracker. The cop stood at the cliff edge south of the blast zone, Tracker was well to the north of it. The cop went down on one knee, pointed at Tracker, and shouted, "Hey!"

Tracker angled down a curved outcropping, part of a massive stone buttress. Going as fast as he dared, he struggled to put the bulk of the towering formation between himself and the hunters above.

"Hey, hey!" The cop who'd first seen him was still shouting, trying to attract attention.

The next cop to get wise was more of a direct actionist than the first. He started shooting as soon as he saw Tracker. He was too far away for his handgun to do anything but break rocks. More cops rushed to the edge and started shooting, sending up a hail of stone chips where their bullets ripped rock. Some of the chips stung the side of Tracker's face, his neck, and arms. He kept angling around the buttress. His flailing feet dislodged loose stones, sending them plummeting. They took a long time to hit bottom.

Once he was careless and missed his hold. He slid helplessly down the face of the cliff for a heart-stopping instant, fingers clawing at stones. His feet hit a narrow ledge, stopping him before he'd fallen more than a body length. A narrow escape, as narrow as the ledge that had saved him.

Some of the cops started whooping when he fell, thinking he'd been hit. The sudden drop put him safely below the sharpshooter's bullet as it tore through the space he'd been occupying a split-second earlier. The riflemen had gotten into play but too late. The narrow ledge spiraled down the rock column. Tracker followed the path around the curve and into the protective lee of the buttress, where the snipers' bullets couldn't reach him. The marksmen would have to take up a new position somewhere above and to the side of him if they wanted their shots to score.

There was a cleft in the rocks on this side of the buttress, a mighty crevasse choked nearly to the brim with shattered stone slabs and loose dirt. A mass of man-high shrubs and even a few tall thin trees put some green in the lower slopes.

Once he reached the top of the cleft, the going was easy. The glutted ravine was a giant stairway. Tracker took it at breakneck speed, leapfrogging from boulder to boulder until he reached level ground. Tracker lurched forward, staggering in the shadows at the base of the cliff. He was covered with cold sweat. His muscles were knotted and aching. Hands and knees were scraped raw, bloody.

Thunder rumbled, shaking the earth. The manmade thunder of a fast-nearing freight train. The noise of its approach was almost a physical presence. The big diesel locomotive at the head of the train came into view as it rounded the curve of the cliff wall. Another locomotive was coupled behind it, and a third was joined to that one. After that came a seemingly endless row of freight cars. The engineer sounded his air horn in a series of warning blasts when he saw Tracker scrambling toward the tracks.

The train was moving along at a nice clip. It was hauling a lot of freight but making good progress as it came barreling into the cut.

The riflemen opened fire from their new vantage point. So did the rest of the cops, but the high-powered scoped rifles were the real threat.

Tracker made use of what cover there was as he ran zigzagging toward the right of way. The cover ended as he neared the gravel railroad bed. That was just what the snipers wanted, for him to show himself in a clear line of fire. Tracker checked, backed up a few steps, and ducked behind a rock. The rock wasn't big, and he had to make himself small to fit in its shelter. He could feel the bullets smashing against the other side.

The engineer figured Tracker for some kind of a crazy who was fixing to get himself killed courtesy of a speeding locomotive. That's what it would take to stop the train, too. It had a schedule to meet and nothing short of a suicidal bum throwing himself under its wheels would delay it. Maybe not even that, if the engineer thought he could get away with claiming later that he hadn't seen a thing. . . .

The engineer didn't see the cops on the cliff, but even if he had, he wouldn't have stopped for them, either. He held down the air horn in one long blast as the train came highballing through the cut. He didn't see the guy on the tracks any more. Probably passed out drunk at the side of the embankment, he thought. At the next instant, just when the engineer thought he could relax, a figure broke from the cover of the underbrush bordering the gravel bed and dashed across the tracks.

Panic made the engineer's heart stand still.

The daredevil maniac cleared the front end of the speeding train with only inches to spare. For a split-second he was so close the engineer could have looked him in the eye if he hadn't been wearing dark glasses.

Hammering sounded against the side of the locomotive. Not until much later, at the end of the line, would the engineer discover that the racket had been made by high-velocity slugs spanging off the steel-plated diesel. Police bullets meant for Tracker. But that was later. For now, the engineer's chilled heart didn't start beating again until he was a hundred yards farther up the tracks. The air horn blasted furiously for the next half-mile as the engineer sounded his rage.

Tracker darted across the rails ahead of the onrushing train and fell into a ditch on the other side. He lay there catching his breath. The train rushed onward. The vacuum of its passing seemed to suck the breath from his lungs. The airstream sprayed him with dust and chaff. Rumbling steel wheels rattled his bones.

He rolled out of the ditch away from the rails and sat up. He was safe from sniper's bullets as long as he stayed in the shelter of the train. Lucky for him it was a long one. The boxcars kept coming like a string of sausage links, one after the other, curving back as far as he could see.

A crewman on a flatcar held onto a safety rail with one hand and gave Tracker the finger with the other. For some reason it made him grin. It helped restore his lack of faith in human nature. Too bad he couldn't hop on board the freight and ride it to safety. But the train was moving too fast. He'd better move fast, too, before he ran out of train and was left out in the open, a sitting duck for sharpshooter's bullets.

East of the tracks was a broad mountain valley, sparsely inhabited. A muddy brown river meandered across it. An iron bridge spanned the water at one point. In the distance were a few widely scattered farms with cultivated fields, barns, silos.

A two-lane blacktop road ran alongside the railroad right of way. Far to the south of the ribbon of road was the sparkling glitter of emergency lights as police cars raced to the scene. They were also-rans. Somebody else had already beaten them to the finish line.

A car stood idling at the bottom of the embankment not more than a stone's throw away from Tracker. It was a beat-up old jalopy that looked like a used car lot's hundred-dollar take-it-or-leave-it special of the week. It hugged the embankment, which was high enough to shield it from the clifftop marksmen. The left front door was open. The driver stood half-in and half-out of the car, urgently beckoning Tracker to join him. He was a dumpy mustached man. A plastic nametag pinned to his shirt-front said, HI I'M GENE.

9.

GENE SAID, "YOU ain't got no shoes on."

"It's the casual look," Tracker said. "How's the hot dog business?"

"Lousy. When the riot broke out, all the bums in the park rushed my stand," Gene said. "Scared hell out of me, all of them coming at me at once. I figured that if they wanted the lunch wagon that bad they could have it."

They were in Gene's car. He was driving, Tracker was in the passenger seat. Gene gave Tracker the onceover out of the corners of his eyes. Tracker put on his socks and shoes.

Gene made a lopsided grin. "Mister, you sure stirred up a hornet's nest! Say, what's your handle, anyhow?"

"Natty. Shades Natty from the Spring."

"From Big Spring, eh?"

"Maybe you've heard of me."

"Yeah, yeah, I think maybe I have," Gene said thoughtfully. "Didn't you use to be a collector for Don Pepe and his bunch?"

"Not me. I don't mob up. I'm independent."

"Tough way to make a buck. These days a guy needs all the friends he can get."

"I get by."

"I'll bet you do, Shades, I'll just bet you do. What's your angle?"

"Troubleshooter."

"Looks like you made your quota today."

"I'm just warming up."

"You're a character. I guess those shades of yours are a trademark or something, eh, Shades?"

"You could say that."

"Pretty fancy. I never saw a pair like that, though."

"Prescription lenses," Tracker said. "I have weak eyes."

The sun was still hours away from setting but it was twilight on the trail Gene's car had taken. A rutted dirt road, little more than a path, snaked through the dismal lowland thickets south of Mountain City. A forest of tall shaggy evergreens blocked most of the sunlight from reaching the pine-needle carpeted ground. Most of the trail tunneled through an arcade of piney boughs.

The murky forest gloom meant nothing to Tracker, who could see through it with his video eyes. He kept squinting through the windshield and sticking his head out the window to see better.

"Get ready for a red-hot scoop, Shades: they killed the wrong guy. Brady didn't rip-off his own bank for millions. He was just a stooge, a straight front man that the real thieves used to make the scam look legit. Then they killed him so he couldn't talk, see?"

"Maybe. Who's 'they'?"

"I could get my ass caught in a sling for talking out of turn. Maybe I've said too much already."

"Suit yourself."

"Don't get sore, Shades."

"Who's sore?"

"I've got to follow the rules, otherwise it's uh-oh time for me. Some things you can't tell to outsiders without an okay from the higher-ups. That's the rule. It's not that I don't trust you, Shades. Hey, anybody who tears into Boyd's bastards like you did is okay in my book. Mitch is going to love you. He's a cop-fighter, too."

"Mitch."

"My boss. You'll be meeting him soon."

"Mitch told you to pick me up?"

"Naw. That was my idea. I used some of that, what do you call it, that individual initiative. Mitch figured that Boyd was going to pull a fast one, so he had the courthouse staked out by some of our boys. That's what I was doing, using the hot dog gimmick as a cover while I kept watch. I spotted you right off.

Something about you said that you had come to kick butt, bigtime.

"After all hell broke loose in the courthouse, one of our scouts tipped me about how the kill had gone down. The riot was going good by then, and I was already in my car, getting ready to pull out. I followed the cops instead, the ones that were chasing you. They thought they had you trapped up there on Northridge. But a guy who rumbles Boyd's goon squad won't let a little thing like a two-hundred-foot drop stymie his getaway. That's how I played it, anyway.

"While the cops were all on Northridge, I went down Farview and turned left at the bottom of the hill. The train came along at about the same time. It was ahead when I started but I passed it. The railroad bed's raised up twenty, maybe thirty feet above the ground. The cops on the cliffs couldn't see my car hugging the wall as I went up the line.

"Then the train came. You cut it pretty close there, Shades. You couldn't have been more than a step or two ahead of the locomotive, but it was enough. You got in my car and we beat it out of there before the cops showed. Gave 'em the slip, too, thanks to this old road I knew about but they didn't," Gene said.

Low branches beat at the windshield and roof. The front bumper mowed down tall weeds growing in the dirt road.

They had escaped, at least temporarily. Tracker knew that for certain because the transceiver built into his opti-visor was monitoring the police radio band. Messages broadcast on the Mountain City police radio net indicated that the cops were still seeking Tracker in the area of the railroad underneath the cliffs. They were cordoning off the area, surrounding it. They thought he was alone, on foot. Boyd's bunch hadn't seen Gene take Tracker away in his car.

"This is an old logging road," Gene said. "Not too many people know about it."

A runner's road, thought Tracker. Contraband runners, hauling booze, drugs, weapons, illegal aliens. Rogues' highway.

Mountain City was built on top of a plateau rising from the two-mile-high rock-ringed basin known as the Kettle. The dirt road snaked through the rugged country east of the base of the plateau. Thick-wooded lowlands, mostly.

The car went deeper into the woods, into the gloomy lowlands. There was a smell of dankness, moist earth, rotting vegetation. Puddles dotted the path.

Wooded hills shaped like giant ant mounds bulked themselves between the path and the Mountain City plateau. At one point the car had to cross a single set of railroad tracks. No structures or roads could be glimpsed through the high walls of greenery bordering the line on both sides. A gap opened in the foliage on the other side of the tracks, marking the continuation of the logger's road. Gene took it. They drove some more. The land started to rise. Tracker saw some power lines and a section of asphalt roadway through a rift in the trees.

"The law'll have all the exits out of the Kettle blocked," he said. "There's a few they don't know about but I do. Besides, who said anything about leaving? We're going to a place where we can lay low for a while, until it's safe for you to meet Mitch."

"You took a pretty big chance, pulling me out of the fire back there."

Gene shrugged. "Not so big. I know every dirt track and billy goat trail in this county. The cops could never catch me."

"If they do, they'll kill us both."

"I can take the heat. I've been around, Shades."

"Got a gun?"

Gene shook his head. "Don't use 'em. I'm no gunman. I never fired a shot in anger in my life. I get by on brains, not bullets."

Gene was telling the truth about not having a gun. Tracker scanned the driver and his car with metal-detecting pulse beams, searching for a weapon, finding none.

They drove some more. A glimmer of brightness at the edge of his shoe caught Tracker's eye. A hard white object about the size of a pearl was embedded in the outer edge of the sole of his boot. It was stuck in pretty deep, but he managed to free it. Holding it between thumb and forefinger, he examined it.

Gene said, "What's that?"

"A tooth."

"Huh?"

"A tooth. Maggard's tooth, I'd say."

"No shit? How do you know that?"

"Because he's the only guy I kicked in the mouth today. One of his teeth must have come loose and stayed stuck in my shoe."

"You sure? Sure you're sure," Gene said, glancing at Tracker. "I never asked you for no favors, Shades, but I'm asking for one now."

"You can always ask."

"Let me have that tooth."

Tracker put the tooth in Gene's extended palm. Gene's fist tightened around it, as if he were afraid of losing it. He held it so tight his knuckles whitened.

"Thanks a million, Shades," he said. With pincerlike fingers he held it up to the light, squinting at it.

"Jeeze, the roots are still bloody," he said. "You're sure this is Maggard's?"

"Try matching it up with the gap in his front teeth the next time you see him, if you don't believe me."

"I believe you."

Gene stowed away the grisly trophy in a cigarette pack, then buttoned the pack inside the breast pocket of his shirt.

"Maggard's tooth," he said. "Talk about a collector's item! Mitch'll pay big bucks for this souvenir! I'll split the take with you, Shades, natch," he added hastily as an afterthought.

"You keep it, it's all yours."

"You mean it? Well, thanks! I can sure use the dough."

"Mitch doesn't much like Maggard, is that right?"

"*Is that right?* Man, Mitch wouldn't piss on him if he was on fire! Well, maybe then, but not until the fire was pretty well out, if you know what I mean."

"I think I do."

"The feeling's mutual with Maggard, too. They hate each other's guts. Put 'em together and they're like two scorpions in a brandy glass. It won't be over until one or both of them is dead. Boyd knows it, too; that's why he won't let Maggard roust Mitch in person, because there's sure to be killing if those two ever go head to head.

"Maggard hates Mitch more than anyone else in the whole wide world. Or at least he did, until you went and kicked out his front teeth for him, Shades. I've got a hunch that the way Maggard feels about Mitch is tame compared to the way he feels about you now."

"I can stand it," Tracker said.

10.

FROM THE NECK up he looked like a mummy, a newly made one with clean white bandages for wrappings.

He was Sgt. Maggard and his head was swathed in antiseptic hospital gauze. Shrouded with bandages from crown to collar, all wrapped up except for eyeholes and a hole for his nose and a narrow horizontal strip at the mouth. His ears were bared and stuck out of the sides of his head like pink flaps.

His broken jaw was wired shut. The bandages were rigged to hold it in place. The upper half of his head was bandaged to anchor the vertical wrappings holding the lower hinge of his jaw in place. His nose was broken, too. A splint was fastened to the bridge of his nose and protected by a triangle-shaped metal nosepiece. Black rings circled his eyes. Puffy flesh swelled out of the openings in the white gauze mask.

Maggard sat on the edge of a cot in an examination room in the emergency ward of Mountain City Hospital. He put on his pants over his shoes. They were baggy pants and didn't give him too much trouble. Standing up did. The effort made him feel like a white-hot railroad spike was being hammered through the hinges of his jaws. What showed of his face turned as white as the gauze. Breath bubbled through clenched teeth.

A big uniformed cop rushed to help him, reaching for his arm. Maggard swatted the other's hands away. The action was almost too much for him. His legs folded, but before he could sink back down to the mattress, he grabbed the iron rail at the foot of the bed and held himself upright.

"Sorry, Sarge," said the big cop, whose nametag identified him as Fenton.

Maggard waved him back. The effort had cost him and he clung to the bedrail, fighting to remain on his feet.

The emergency ward was crowded this evening. From outside the room came a chorus of pain, mingling the cries of the injured with the clamor of their concerned friends and relatives. The courthouse riot had produced a bumper crop of casualties, swamping the hard-pressed hospital staffers. Maggard's immediate treatment and private recovery room proved his clout, and that of Boyd, who had seen to the arrangements.

Maggard shook off a fainting spell and closed his pants with shaking hands. Bands of muscle stood out on his chest and shoulders as he struggled into his blue shirt. He left it open, unbuttoned.

He saw himself in a wall-mounted mirror. He went to it, shuffling like a shaky old man. The mirror was mounted on the wall behind a stainless steel sink. Maggard held the edge of the sink for support and leaned forward, peering into the mirror. After a time, Maggard's heavy breathing slowed, deepened. He was immobile, not moving a muscle. Letting out a breath, he straightened up and let go of the sink.

The door opened and a doctor came into the room. Another cop stood in the hall. He closed the door from the outside. The doctor wore a nametag, too, a black plastic one with white lettering that was pinned to the front of his white lab coat. He was Dr. Beckley, a young doctor who wore a mustache to look older. He got upset when he saw Maggard on his feet. "See here, what do you think you're doing out of bed? You're in no condition to be walking around, you need complete rest!"

Beckley took Maggard by the arm to lead him back to bed. Maggard, snarling, grabbed a double fistful of the doctor's shirtfront, swung him around, and slammed him against the wall. The doctor cried out, more in fear than in pain. Maggard shook him.

"Please, don't!" Beckley said.

The cop outside opened the door and stuck his head in the room.

"It's okay," Fenton said.

The other cop withdrew, closed the door.

Maggard bounced the medic around a few more times, then released him. Beckley slid down the wall and sat down on the floor, cowering. He flinched at a sudden move by Maggard but Maggard was only reaching into his pants pockets, searching for something.

No cop is ever without his notepad and Maggard was no exception. He took his out of a pocket and flipped it open to a blank page and started writing on it with a pen that had been clipped onto the pad. He scrawled something and shoved the pad near the doctor's face so he could read the message. It was a single word: PAINKILLERS. It was underlined three times and followed by three exclamation points.

Beckley said, "You're liable to do yourself permanent damage—"

Maggard grabbed the other's torn shirtfront and shook him again, then waved the message in front of his face.

"Best do like he says, Doc," Fenton said, not unkindly. "When the sarge gets his mind set on something, there's no stopping him."

"He could suffer a serious relapse without proper treatment. Possibly a fatal one. He might die!"

"It won't be Sarge who does the dying. So be smart and get something to fix him up like he told you."

Maggard lifted Beckley to his feet with one hand. White gauze contrasted with eyes as black and hard and shiny as two lumps of coal.

"I'll do it," Beckley said.

Maggard unfisted the other's shirt and tried to smooth it out.

"But I won't be responsible for the consequences!"

Maggard didn't even bother to shrug.

As Beckley slunk off, Fenton called after him, "That's playing it smart, Doc."

Maggard tore out the used piece of paper from the notepad, crumpled it up and threw it away. He made a new entry on a fresh page and showed it to Fenton. The scrawled message, triply underlined, read: MY GUN!!!

Tracker waited out the daylight hours at the hideout to which Gene had taken him. It was an old, abandoned firewatch tower in a long wooded valley. After dark, Gene took him to Redrow to meet Mitch.

Redrow was in the south ward of Mountain City, nestled in a hollow near the edge of the city limits. The hollow stretched east–west. Rowe Street, its main thoroughfare, ran down the middle of it, more of a broad avenue than a street. The median was an old abandoned railway line that spanned the length of the central strip. It was a common saying that both sides of Rowe Street were on the wrong side of the tracks.

It was a slum, dirty and dangerous, the toughest piece of turf in Mountain City—in the Kettle. Blocks of heavy stone tenements, a hundred years old, laid out on a gridwork of cracked narrow streets. Streetlights here seemed fewer and dimmer than anywhere else in the city. Billboards hawked booze, cigarettes, topless bars, 24-hour bail bond services. There was a gin mill on every corner, each equipped with its full quota of hookers, hustlers, and hangers-on. Their action spilled off the sidewalks into the streets.

When Mountain City folk had a yen for illicit thrills, Redrow is where they went to find them.

The streets were clogged with traffic, especially along the Strip, the heart of the vice district. Most of the cars belonged to outsiders cruising for hookers or drugs or both. There was a frantic carnival atmosphere, as if today's outbreak of riots and murder had set loose some long-restrained urge to wildness among the citizenry.

Gene drove away from the Strip's neon rainbow lights. A hooker staggered in front of the car. Gene had to hit the brakes hard to keep from hitting her. She was wasted. She put her palms on the hood of the car, holding herself up, head hanging down. Gene honked the horn. Her head lifted, face underlit by the headlights so that it looked like something out of a nightmare. Under the too-heavy makeup, she was young. Fifteen going on fifty. The street ages them fast.

"Move!" Gene said.

She told Gene what he could do to himself, that is, if he wasn't too busy doing it to his mother instead.

"I'll run your ass over."

Gene eased the car ahead at a few miles per hour. Seeing that he wasn't kidding, the hooker stumbled to the curb, shrieking obscenities. She was holding a pint bottle of cheap wine, the high-alcohol kind that gives the lushes the kick they crave. She wasn't so drunk that she didn't check to make sure it was empty before chucking it. The spinning bottle glittered as it sped toward the open window on Tracker's side. He put up a hand and caught it in midair, the bottle smacking snugly into his palm.

The hooker stood in the gutter, staring open-mouthed as the car's taillights dwindled. When it was gone she turned and tripped on the curb and fell, breaking off one of her high heels.

Tracker flipped the empty into the next streetside trash barrel that came along. They were few and far between.

Gene said, "Man, how'd you catch that? You must have eyes in the back of your head!"

"I need them in this town."

"Nice neighborhood, huh? I live about five blocks away from here. I'm a Redrow boy, born and bred. Never lived anywhere else in my life. Mitch is from Redrow, too. So are most of the boys in the outfit. Maggard, too."

"Somehow that doesn't surprise me," Tracker said.

Sgt. Bob Martinez of the Colorado Springs Police Department was working late in his office tonight. He'd stayed on for a few hours after his regular shift went off-duty. A backlog of paperwork was cluttering his desk, and he wanted to clear some of it off. There were reports to be typed, forms to be filled out, files needing updates, and cases to be closed.

Among his other duties, Martinez was the department's liaison to his counterparts in the military police security force at the NORAD facility in nearby Cheyenne Mountain. It was literally *in* the mountain, which had been hollowed out to house the extensive installation. It was a vital link in the global chain of EMG sentinels guarding the nation from sneak enemy attacks.

Piles of paperwork hid the framed plaques and citations awarded for heroism in the line of duty, crowding them to the desktop's edge. Document by document, Martinez chipped away at the workload. By eight that night, he'd had enough. He decided to call it a day and knock off early. For him, leaving at eight was early. He got his hat and coat, turned off the lights, locked the office door. He was square-jawed and solidly built, with salt-and-pepper hair and mustache. The big-bore gun in his shoulder holster made a bulge a little smaller than a steam iron.

He walked with a heavy tread. The desk sergeant heard him

coming down the hall and knew who it was long before he saw him. The desk sergeant was in the middle of a phone conversation. His assistant said, low-voiced, "Here comes Bullet Bob. Give it to him."

"Good idea," the desk sergeant said. Then he spoke into the phone: "Please hold for a minute." He covered the mouthpiece with his hand and called Martinez over to the desk.

"What's up?" Martinez said.

The desk sergeant said, "You know a guy named Tracker, an Air Force dude?"

"Sure, I know him. Man's a friend of mine. That him on the line?"

"No, it's some Mountain City dick asking about him."

"Mountain City?" Martinez's shaggy eyebrows lifted. "Wonder what Natty's doing up there?"

The desk sergeant shrugged.

"Let me talk to him," Martinez said, going around to the side of the desk. He climbed three steps and went behind the desk. "That Natty!" he said, chuckling. "He's a good old boy, but he's one of those amateur detectives who thinks that he can crack the cases that are just too tough for us poor dumb cops."

"He probably couldn't do any worse than those Mountain City clowns," the desk sergeant said, after checking that the phone's mouthpiece was still completely covered by his hand.

"Not that he hasn't helped me out on one or two cases," Martinez added, reaching for the phone. "I did all the work, of course, but he came up with a couple of lucky hunches that helped me clinch the investigations."

"Of course."

Martinez gave him a hard look, but the desk sergeant stayed poker-faced so Martinez couldn't tell if he was being needled or not. He took the phone. A voice at the other end of the line said, "This is Detective Monty of the Mountain City police department."

"Sgt. Martinez here."

"We'd appreciate your cooperation in an ongoing investigation of ours, Sergeant. We need any information you've got on an individual residing in your locality: last name Tracker, first name Nathaniel, middle initial unknown to us at this time."

"What's that rascal gone and done now?"

"He's wanted for a couple of murders, for starters. Plus resisting arrest, assaulting a police officer, auto theft, reckless driving, leaving the scene of an accident, destruction of municipal property, and trespassing on a railroad right of way."

"What?"

"That's the gist of it, leaving out the minor charges," Monty said. "We want this hotshot flyboy pretty badly up here. Nobody's safe while this menace is on the loose."

11.

SCANNING THE RADIO waves, Tracker sampled random snatches of messages broadcast on the Citizen's Band channel:

"Breaker 1-9, Breaker 1-9, can somebody give me a 10-20 on the Smoky roadblock west of Loghouse Road—"

"Any of you big truckers hauling a hot load of freight, come on down to the rest area a half-mile south of the Seventy-Six truckstop and ask for Bodacious Kate and Ruby Redlips, that's us, we'll put your hammers down and make 'em stand right back up again—"

"Teddy Bear calling Phantom 3-0-9, come in?"

Nothing for him there. Tracker switched over to the police radio net:

Auto accident at the intersection of Dain and Cooper streets. Convenience store robbed on Schuyler. Fire at 1101 North Frontier Drive, an apartment building. Teacher's car vandalized in the high school parking lot. Convenience store robbed on Kimbrough Street. Reported drunk and disorderly persons outside Graney's Lounge. Domestic disturbance at the Wellfleet Projects. Another convenience store robbed in a different part of town. Wanted for murder—

He locked in on that one.

"Attention all units, attention all units, be on the lookout for Nathaniel Tracker, wanted for multiple murder in the gangland-style slayings of two men at City Courthouse earlier today. He is believed to be armed and is extremely dangerous. Tracker is a

martial arts expert able to kill with his hands and feet. All units are instructed that no attempt is to be made to apprehend Tracker. He's to be shot on sight, repeat, shot on sight. Don't take any chances with this one, people, he's a mad dog killer."

Palladium Bowlarama was built back in the days when they were called bowling alleys, not bowling lanes. Since then, bowling had gone upmarket, but the Palladium stayed in the alley. No matter what it was called, the Palladium's best days were long gone. Outsiders didn't come to Redrow to bowl, and the locals had other ways to occupy their time.

The Palladium was the main attraction of a shabby little mini-mall a half-mile east of the strip on Rowe. It was a long shedlike concrete block building with an arched roof. It stood off by itself, with its short end fronting Rowe Street. Off to one side was a strip of small shops including a dry cleaner, Chinese restaurant, and a card and gift shop. The shops were all closed. Tracker couldn't tell if they were closed for the night or if they'd gone permanently out of business.

At first glance, the Palladium looked like it was closed, too. Its neon sign was dark, and the front entrance was boarded up with sheets of plywood. But there were some lights on inside, and a few parked cars were clustered down at the opposite end of the building. Tracker's scanners detected no unusual activity, no signs of a trap, no police or other hostile life forms lurking in ambush. An EMG sweep searching for the intense ionization and coronal phenomena caused by the energization of the lightning ball also came up negative.

Gene said, "Pretty slick, huh? The cops'll never think of looking for you in a bankrupt bowling joint." He parked near the other cars at the back of the building. "Better let me do the talking, Shades, at least till we get inside."

"Sure."

"Mitch ain't a bad guy but he's got some real hardheads working for him."

They crossed to a side door in the middle of one of the building's long sides. Tracker slouched to hide his height. A baseball cap with a PETER-BILT truck company logo was pulled down low over his face. He also wore a Batman T-shirt and a dark blue lightweight nylon jacket. Gene had picked up the cap and the change of clothes earlier, buying them at a convenience store while Tracker waited outside in the car. Clean new clothes were a morale booster and a pretty good disguise, too.

A narrow sidewalk stuck out in front of the side door like a concrete tongue. The door opened as soon as Tracker and Gene set foot on the path. Yellow light slanted through the open doorway. Two men followed it outside. "That's Reese and Cole working the door," Gene said, talking out of the side of his mouth like a con in a prison yard. "Hard guys," he added unnecessarily, since Tracker could see that both men were big, strong, and tough.

The first one outside said, "Well, look who's here!"

"Hey, Reese. Cole," Gene said, nodding to the other.

"Sledge has got a real mad on about you, boy," Cole said.

"Sledge? Is he inside?"

"Yeah. I sure hope you're here to pay him off for his hot dog wagon that you ruined today. I hope so, for your sake."

"Mitch here?"

"What's it to you, squirt?" Reese said, sneering.

"I got to talk to him."

"You? The likes of you's got no business with Mitch."

"I've got to see him, it's important."

"Everybody wants to see Mitch and it's always important."

"Maybe the squirt wants to hit him up for a loan to pay off Sledge," Cole suggested.

"I'd be out on my ass with the rest of the bums if I let in every mutt who wants to hit up Mitch for a touch," Reese said. "On your way, squirt. G'wan, blow."

"You'll be out on your ass if you don't let me in," Gene said, standing his ground.

"You got a big mouth, little man."

"He's showing off for his pal," Cole said, meaning Tracker.

"What I've got, Mitch wants," Gene said. "If he doesn't get it, he'll have your heads on a platter."

"You got a nasty mouth, too," Reese said, starting forward. "Guess I'll have to shut it for you."

Cole put a hand on the other's shoulder, stopping him. "Easy, Reese. The squirt wouldn't be smarting off to us if he didn't have something. Maybe we better pass him through at that."

"You won't be sorry."

"You will, if you can't deliver the goods. I'll take you apart myself, if Sledge don't do it first. All right, go on in."

"Thanks, Reese. He's with me," Gene said, indicating Tracker.

"No way. I don't know him from Adam."

"I'll vouch for him a hundred and ten per cent."

"So what? Your okay don't cut no ice with nobody, squirt."

"I need him, he's part of the deal."

"Hell, Reese, let both of them in. It's all on the squirt's neck if it don't pan out anyway," Cole said.

"Nice guys," Tracker said when they were inside.

"Not really. All they are is muscle. Screw 'em," Gene said.

"I heard that, squirt," Cole said. But he didn't do anything about it. He and Reese stayed at their post, manning the door.

Inside, the Palladium was cavernous, gloomy, barnlike. None of the fifteen lanes was in use. To the left of the door as they came in there was a setback space holding a bar, stools, a row of booths with tables and chairs, and two pool tables. It smelled of tobacco smoke and beer. Three men sat in one of the booths, drinking and talking. Two others were playing pool and a third kibitzed. A very big man and an average-sized big man sat on stools at the bar. Hard men all.

The bartender wore a white shirt with the sleeves rolled up and a black bow tie. His lined pink face was as professionally composed as a mortician's. He was the first in the bar to see Gene and Tracker. He looked up from the countertop he was polishing with a limp rag, glanced at the newcomers, and looked down again without saying a word or moving a muscle in his face.

Gene halted, saying, "Uh-oh, it's Sledge."

"Who's he?"

The big man at the bar saw Gene, turned, and nudged his companion, the very big man. The very big man's face lit up.

Gene tried to brazen it out. Squaring his shoulders, assuming a jauntiness he could not be feeling, he breezed up to the bar. He said, "Hey, Dudley, is Mitch around?"

"Mitch who?" the bartender said.

"What are you putting me on for? You know who I mean. *Mitch*!" Dudley shrugged.

A bar stool scraped on the floor as it was pushed back away from the counter. The very big man got off it and stood up. He said, "So you decided to come back and take your medicine, huh, squirt?"

Tracker asked Gene, "That's Sledge?"

"Yeah."

"The biggest guy in the place. Figures."

Sledge came toward them, blotting out much of the background. He reminded Tracker of why strongarm goons are often called gorillas.

Gene backpedaled, holding up his hands in front of him. "The bums hit that wagon like a flock of locusts, Sledge. There was nothing I could do!"

"You fucked up and I'm out a wagon bcause of it," Sledge said.

"I'll make it good, Sledge, I swear."

"I knew you'd fuck things up, that's why I didn't want to let you use one of my wagons in the first place. But Mitch said do it, so I did it, now I'm the loser."

"I'll make good!"

"With what? You ain't got a pot to piss in. I got to eat the cost of a new wagon, but at least I'll mop up the floor with you."

Tracker said, "How much is Gene into you for?"

"Gene? You mean the squirt here? Who wants to know?"

"I'll cover your losses."

"You will, huh? Who're you? Who let this goof in here?"

"Don't blame me," Reese called from over by the side door. "It was all the squirt's idea."

Tracker felt himself starting to lose patience. He fought to hold his temper. "Look, do you want the money or not?" he said.

"Watch me give this guy enough rope," Sledge said to his friend at the bar. He said to Tracker, "Yeah, I want the money. You got it?"

"How much?"

"Ten thousand bucks, bigshot."

"I saw that wagon. It wasn't worth more than two thousand."

"Sounds like he's calling you a liar, Sledge," the guy at the bar said.

"Shut up, Connor," Sledge said. "Let this guy finish digging himself into a hole."

"I'll give you three thousand. That'll cover your losses and give you a nice profit, too," Tracker said.

"Let's see the dough, big spender."

"I don't have it with me, but I can get it."

"I've heard that song before," Sledge said. "Another chiseler, huh? I'll start by taking you apart first, wiseguy."

Sledge reached for Tracker. Tracker side-stepped, grabbing Sledge's wrist with one hand. The wrist was as thick as the average man's ankle. Tracker couldn't get his fingers all the way around it. But it didn't matter. Sledge had been moving forward. Tracker helped him along with a judo-style throw. When he let go of Sledge's wrist, it was like releasing the last one in line in a game of snap-the-whip. Sledge hurtled forward, colliding with a table and some chairs, overturning them. He fell over the top of the table and tumbled headfirst across the floor until he fetched up against the wall with a crash.

Conner grabbed his heavy beer mug and raised it to brain Tracker as he rushed him from behind. Tracker nailed him with a back thrust kick, planting his booted foot deep into Connor's belly. Connor folded, flying backward until he slammed into the pool table. Connor sat down on the floor with his legs sticking out. His mouth was an open moaning hole that took up half his pale, bloodless face. Hugging his middle, he rocked back and forth.

Sledge got up, shaking himself off. A chair was tangled with one of his feet, and he gave it an irritated little kick that sent it flying halfway across the room. "Cute," he said, "but if that's your best trick, you're in trouble."

"It's not," Tracker said.

"You're in trouble anyhow. You put a hand on Sledge. No man does that and lives."

"Take it outside," Dudley said. "You know Mitch doesn't want any trouble in here."

"Won't be no trouble. It's gonna be a massacre," Sledge said.

"I was thinking the same thing," Tracker said.

Gene took advantage of the diversion to dart across the floor to the far end of the booths, where he disappeared around a corner into an alcove.

"I'm gonna show you why they call me 'Sledge.' " Sledge raised his fists chest-high. They were as big as paving stones. He brought down his right fist on top of the nearest table, hammering it. The tabletop split in two. Both halves fell away from each other and hit the floor.

"You're pretty good against tables, but they don't hit back," Tracker said.

"I'll tell them you died game," Sledge said, coming toward him.

Dudley reached for something under the bar. "Aw, let 'em fight," said one of the men in the booth.

"We could use some laughs around here," another said.

Dudley began, "But Mitch says—"

"Mitch says, let 'em fight," a new voice said. It was the voice of command.

Mitch's voice.

Mitch stood in the aisle between the booths and the pool tables, with Gene and a serious dark-bearded man standing near him. "Let 'em fight," he said again.

"Okay, Mitch," Dudley said, putting his empty hands back on top of the bar.

Mitch was fiftyish, with an iron-gray flattop crewcut and arched Satanic eyebrows of the same color. His face was wider than it was long. He was barrel-chested, with a bull neck and thick shoulders and arms. The matted chest hair curling out of the top of his open-necked sportshirt was iron-gray, too. Smoke curled from the tip of the foot-long cigar stuck in the corner of his mouth.

Connor still sat on the floor, propped up against the side of the pool table, hugging himself and gasping.

"He don't sound too good," Mitch said, taking the cigar out of his mouth so he could flick ashes on Connor's head. He gestured it at Tracker and Sledge. "Well, what are you waiting for?" he said. "Get to it!"

"I'll be done in a jiffy, boss," Sledge said, moving forward.

The bearded man said, "How about some action, Mitch?"

"I'm game. I'll put five hundred on the stranger to win."

"You're throwing your money away."

"Izzat so? Make it a grand, then."

"Betting against me, Mitch? That ain't smart," Sledge said.

Ignoring him, Mitch pressed the bearded man: "A grand on the stranger to win. We got a bet or not, Vee?"

"I don't know. Now I'm thinking that maybe you know something I don't here."

"Ain't that the truth. Come on, make up your mind."

"Five hundred on Sledge."

"Hedging your bet, Vee? Okay, I'll take your five."

One of the pool players who'd been standing around with a

cue in his hands doing nothing since Connor had ruined the game, said, "I want to get in on some of this. Can I put a thousand on Sledge?"

"You can put two thousand on him."

"You got it, Mitch."

Gene said, "I'll take another two grand of Shades' action if you're game, Red."

"What'll you pay off with if you lose? Hot dogs?" the red-headed pool player said sneering.

"His marker's good."

"The squirt's? You ribbing me, Mitch?"

"No, Red. I got him covered if he loses, which he ain't gonna."

"That's good enough for me, Mitch. Okay, little man, you're faded. Easy come, easy go."

"Make it five thousand then, if you've got the guts," Gene said.

Red looked to Mitch, who nodded, saying, "But no more than five grand."

"Suits me," Red said, shrugging. "I can use the dough. Okay, squirt, shoot the works. Five thousand it is."

"Just make sure you can pay off in full when you lose," Gene said.

"This guy just don't know when to quit," Red said, laughing, shaking his head, unsure whether to be irritated or amused. He thought Sledge was a sure thing so he decided to be amused.

Sledge, unamused, advanced on Tracker. He held his arms out from his sides, as if to forestall any attempt by Tracker to slip past him and away. He moved clumsily, like a trained bear walking on its hind legs, but a solid swipe from one of his hands could smash a man's skull as easily as if it were a honeycomb.

Tracker rushed him, jumped up into a flying front kick, and kicked Sledge in the chest. Sledge cannonballed backward, opening up some much-needed room to maneuver for Tracker.

Sledge could take it. He lurched to a stop a dozen paces away, still on his feet. His chest heaved but his eyes were glowing and he was grinning.

"Why don't you quit that kicking and fight like a man?" he said.

"Sad," Tracker said, shaking his head, walking toward Sledge. He had not taken off his opti-visor. It would stay in place throughout his greatest exertions, and if he were struck in the head, the unbreakable polycarbonate view screen would protect his video eyes.

Sledge came shuffling forward, massive arms held in a boxer's peekaboo style to protect his head and chest. At the last instant before they closed, Tracker lashed out with a side snap kick that broke Sledge's left kneecap.

Sledge collapsed with one of his pins knocked out from under him. He fell sideways and rolled off the edge of a platform, onto the hardwood floor between the bar area and the lanes. He landed on his back with a plop. His face was white, agonized. He clenched his teeth, bit down. His face reddened, veins stood out on his hand, his neck was a mass of straining tendons. He raised himself on one elbow.

"That's all there is to it," Tracker said.

"Yeah?" Sledge said, thrusting a hand into his jacket pocket, splitting the seams as he groped for something.

"Don't."

"The hell with this fair-fight bullshit," Sledge said. His hand closed on an object in his pocket. Tracker grabbed a bowling ball off a rack and threw it at him, then dodged to one side.

"No—!"

Sledge's shout was cut off by the bowling ball smashing into his chest, hammering him to the hardwood floor. Convulsively he jerked the trigger of the gun in his pocket, drilling a hole in the wall.

The ball rolled across a lane and into the gutter.

"Whoa," somebody said at last.

"Satisfied?" Tracker said, not breathing hard.

"I am," Mitch said, grinning. "I just made me twenty-five hundred bucks on you, Shades."

"And I made five grand!" Gene said.

"The hell is this, a fight or a bowling match?" Red groused, sullen.

"What's the diff? You bet on Sledge to win. He lost. Pay up."

"I ain't so sure about that, Mitch."

"Get sure," the man named Vee said.

"You crazy, Vollin? You lost, too!"

"That's right, Red, I did, and you don't hear me bellyaching about it."

"Easy for you to say. You're only out five hundred, I'm out seven thousand bucks!"

"I'm no gambler, Red. That's not how I make my money." Vee Vollin rested his hands on the twin .45s he wore stuffed into the top of his waistband, butt-first. "*This* is how I make my money," he said, "and I hate welshers."

"I never welshed on a bet in my life!"

"So quit whining and pay up."

"Sure, Vee, sure. I was just bitching, didn't mean nothing by it. I'm going to reach in my pocket now to get my dough, that's all, just wanted to tell you first, Vee."

"I appreciate the consideration."

Red was a gambler and carried a wad of bills big enough to choke a horse. He carried a gun for protection, too, but he kept his hands as far away from it as he could while he counted out Mitch's money.

"Him, too," Vollin said, indicating Gene.

"*Him?* I mean, sure thing, Vee, whatever you say."

"Whatever's right."

"Sure, Vee."

Dudley put both hands on the counter, leaned far over the bar, and cleared his throat. Almost apologetically, he said, "What about Sledge?"

"What about him?" Mitch said. "Damn, my cigar went out."

"Is he dead? Sledge, I mean."

"He better be, after costing me seven grand," Red said.

"Go check," Mitch said to the men in the booth. All three got up, two went to examine Sledge, the other sat down.

The two knelt beside the body.

"Dead," one of them said after a moment.

"Deader than hell," said the other.

"Like this cigar," Mitch said. "Who's got a light?"

The third man got up from the table and held the flame of a lighter to the end of Mitch's cigar as Mitch huffed and puffed to get it going.

The kibitzer who'd been watching the pool game earlier now went to take a closer look at Sledge's corpse. "Bowling ball? Looks more like he got hit with a cannonball!" he said.

Dudley said, "What about the body, Mitch?"

"Worried you're gonna lose your liquor license, Dud?" said the man who had lit Mitch's cigar. "Christ, you fuss like an old lady. You'd think you were tending bar at the Sunday brunch at the Holiday Inn or something."

"Big talk, Burgos!" Red spots of color burned in Dudley's cheeks. "A fine fix we'd be in if the cops walked in now and saw Sledge smeared all over the floor!"

"A fine fix *they'd* be in," Mitch said, breaking the tension. Some of the others laughed, Burgos too loudly.

"But Dud's right, like always. That's why I keep him around. It sure ain't on account of how he mixes drinks, I can tell you that. Get rid of the body, pronto."

"The usual way, Mitch?"

"Unless you'd rather eat it instead, Tully."

"Hah hah hah, that's a good one, Mitch."

"Shut up, Burgos. No, don't say anything, just shut it."

Burgos nodded, his lips tightly closed.

Mitch jabbed his cigar like an accusing finger at Cole and Reese. "Some lookouts you are," he said. "How're you going to see anything from here, you morons? Get back where you belong." Cole and Reese took off at a run for their post at the side door.

"I've got an idea, Mitch," Vollin said. "Why not just leave Sledge here and burn the place down? That way we kill two birds with one stone. We get rid of the body, and we collect the insurance on this dump. It's a firetrap anyway."

"Yeah, and we can knock off a bunch of guys we don't like all at once and burn them up, too. A fire sale, if you get me."

"I thought I told you to shut up, Burgos."

"Sorry, Mitch."

"Not that that's such a bad idea," Mitch added after a moment's thought.

"Too complicated," Vollin said. "One body you can explain. Say he's the dope who started the fire and got burned up by it. Too many bodies would queer the insurance claim."

"Forget it," Dudley said. "We're not insured. The company that wrote the policy went kaput last week. That means no payoff on claims. Sorry."

"Damn! The bastards get you coming and going," Vollin said.

"Sorry."

"You see the trouble you put me to?" Mitch said to Tracker. "You wanted a fight, you got it."

"I got twenty-five hundred bucks worth of winnings out of it, too. Not bad, and the night's young. This could be the start of a profitable association."

"For you, maybe," Tucker said. "So far I haven't made a penny."

"Don't kid me, Major. A guy like you ain't in it for the money," Mitch said, smiling a secret smile.

The "Major" reference was not lost on Tracker.

"I ain't so dumb," Mitch said. "Suppose we step into my office for a little private chat."

"Let's," Tracker said.

12.

MITCH'S OFFICE HAD formerly belonged to the Palladium's onetime manager. There were gray metal filing cabinets and a brown plastic wood desk. Instead of a swivel chair behind the desk, there was a full-sized, overstuffed recliner lounge chair that would have seemed more at home in a den facing the TV. One wall was hung with thick dark curtains. Tracker looked at them. "Window?" he said.

"Give me credit for a little brains at least," Mitch said. "Yeah, there's a window. There's also a sheet of bullet-proof steel behind the curtains, too."

"I thought it was stuffy in here."

"That's my cigar. Want one?"

"No, thanks."

"Good. They ain't cheap." Mitch went around behind the desk and flopped into his relaxer. "Ah, it's so good to get back in my chair! I hate to get out of it."

Tracker looked around. The other three walls were covered with framed certificates, plaques, photos of long-forgotten bowling stars of yesteryear.

"It's America's fastest growing sport," Mitch said. "Bowling, I mean."

"In this town, I thought it was murder."

"Ha ha. Sit down and make yourself comfortable."

Tracker sat on the edge of Mitch's desk, leaning over him. "Let's talk," he said.

"I know who you are, Major Tracker, U.S. Air Force. Yeah, I know who you are, and so do the cops. They wrung it out of the grieving widow of your pal Purdy." Seeing Tracker's angry start, Mitch held up his hand, as if to pacify him. "Relax. They didn't hurt her. The way I heard it, she was so numbed by shock that she answered anything they asked her without knowing what she was saying.

"No, I know who you are, Major. It's *what* you are that puzzles me. I ain't figured it out yet, but I got me some pretty good ideas on the subject."

"And you? What're you, Mitch?"

Mitch pressed a button on a console inset on one of the arms of his chair. There was a whirring sound as an electric motor hidden somewhere in the recliner tilted Mitch so he was sitting straight up. He put his elbows on the desktop and leaned forward. "I'll tell you what I am. I'm a businessman," Mitch said. "Why are you laughing? It's not funny."

"I'm not laughing."

"You don't want to piss me off, Major. I'm the best friend you got in this town, not to mention the onliest."

"You're a businessman? Talk business."

"Okay. I heard from my sources about what you done at the courthouse today. Even allowing for it to be about ninety per cent bullshit, the fact remains that you kicked some kind of major league ass out there today. The ass you were kicking belongs to the guys who've been kicking my ass. You handled Boyd's goons like they were a bunch of kids, and they ain't no pushovers. Then there's the way you bowled a strike on poor dumb Sledge. I know a pro when I see one, Major, and you're a pro. A pro killer."

He looked at Tracker for a reaction.

"You're telling it," Tracker said.

"Who're you working for? Somebody big. Federal, maybe. Not the FBI, though. If a G-man ever tore up a town like you've been doing, old J. Edgar Hoover would be turning in his grave. You ain't mob, either. I can see that at a glance. You just ain't got the style. Corporate hitman, maybe. Some of those big business types keep their own private killers on the payroll. It ain't too much of a stretch to picture you as one of those."

"You flatter me."

"But the military connection is the tip-off. That worries me.

What's the Air Force doing rumbling with crooked cops in Mountain City? Uh-uh, it don't figure. The military bit is just a cover."

"I'm retired from active duty, Mitch."

"Like I said, a perfect cover. You're into something bigger than that. Oh, I dunno, the flyboys might be part of it, but only part. I figure it's one of those spy things. Top secret bullshit. Some kind of CIA operation or something."

"The CIA's not allowed to operate inside the U.S., Mitch."

"Who's kidding who?"

"I don't suppose you'd believe me if I told you I only came to Mountain City to help out a friend."

"Sure, sure, anything you say. Well, now you can help out another friend: me. I know the guys you want and I'll help you get 'em."

"Careful you don't bite off more than you can chew."

"What have I got to lose? If I don't fight back I'm dead meat anyway. Listen, Major, I didn't get where I am today by not being able to keep my mouth shut. You don't want to tell me who you're working for, fine. I don't want to know. Some things a guy is better off not knowing. Look at Johnny Rosselli and Momo. They knew too much about some gigs the mob pulled for the super-spooks who really run this country, so what happened? They got their lips zipped permanently. Not me, boy. What I don't know won't hurt me. I don't want some superspy kill-master coming after me—somebody like you."

"You've got me all wrong, Mitch. I'm no spy and no killer. I know you don't believe it, but it's true."

"Hey, I don't care, Major. Whatever you say is all right with me, just so long as we're working together."

Tracker sighed.

"That a yes?" Mitch said eagerly.

"Let's hear what you've got."

Mitch was a hood, the boss of the crime mob that ruled Redrow. That meant that he ran the rackets in Mountain City. A traditional-type mobster, he stuck to the tried and true standards of organized crime: narcotics, prostitution, gambling, extortion, and union politics. Among other things, he was vice president of the local chapter of one of the most powerful labor unions in the West, the Rocky Mountain Mining Heavy Equipment Operators and Transporters Union. The president of the local was a pliable nitwit, a figurehead who could be thrown to the wolves as a fall guy if needed.

Organized crime can't succeed without police protection. That was Lt. Boyd's contribution to the team. Boyd was the boss of a ring of crooked cops at all levels throughout the department. Boyd was the smoothie. Sgt. Maggard was his enforcer. Maggard ran a wrecking crew, a goon squad of corrupt cops. Whenever somebody was dumb or greedy enough to try to set up their own rackets without an official okay, Maggard and his men would put them out of business and into the jailhouse hospital, sometimes the morgue when one of the crew got a little carried away.

The system worked. Trouble came in the form of W. Carson Yates.

"God wants *you* to be rich." This was the slogan indelibly linked to Yates in the minds of millions of insomniac TV watchers who'd seen any of his series of late-night, half-hour-long infomercials. He was one of the most successful of the new breed of money barkers spawned during the last decade, combining the fervor of an oldtime evangelist with a get-rich-quick gospel.

Yates' beginnings were in the cutthroat market of lease sales in the Oklahoma oil patch. He'd gone west in search of richer pickings, making his first significant money buying and selling mineral property rights during the faddish shale oil craze that followed the shock of the first Arab oil embargo. The bubble burst fast, but not before Yates had sold short and made a killing in the market. That supplied the capital for his subsequent investments.

Success followed success in his dazzling career as a high-flying, risk-taking entrepreneur. He expanded into real estate, banking, and commodities ventures. At the same time, he went public with a big splash by launching his Mega-Millionaire Wealth-Generating Program, blitzing late-night TV with his relentless half-hour commercials. Millions of dollars worth of audio and video cassettes, workbooks, and seminars purportedly revealing his secret money-making techniques were sold throughout the fifty states.

Kublai Khan had his Xanadu, Louis XIV his Versailles, Hearst his San Simeon. Ultima was W. Carson's Yates' architectural white elephant, a fantastically expensive and self-indulgent folly.

Ultima was supposed to be the ultimate planned community, a luxurious retreat for the world-class rich who simply couldn't bear to rub elbows with grubby mere millionaires at Aspen. In design, Ultima resembled a Swiss mountain village, a futuristic version rendered in steel and glass, isolated, restricted, ultra-secure. It would be built on Oldridge, a natural shelf on the middle heights of the mountains ringing the Kettle.

Ultima was to be Yates' showpiece, the crown jewel of his far-flung financial empire. He set up headquarters in nearby Mountain City so he could personally oversee the construction. A sense of near-hysterical excitement seized most of the citizenry, thrilled by the presence of the world-famous mega-millionaire. When Yates' flagship Seven Cities company opened a branch office in Mountain City, it was like the day Howard Hughes came to Las Vegas.

Yates had been one of the pioneers in the junk bond mania that hit the investment community like a shot of cocaine. Seven Cities' impressive financial performance was built on a mountain of junk bonds, paper assets, and bad debts. This true state of affairs was kept carefully concealed from the shareholders until well after the company crashed.

But that came later. At first, Seven Cities looked as good as gold. Better, since the early investors were regularly doubling their money. They redoubled their investments on the next round, while envious others who hadn't gotten in on the first dividends flocked to buy shares lest they miss the next big payout. Even the most fiscally conservative types got on board for fear of missing the bus.

It was a scam, of course, a mega-swindle. The modern trappings of hostile takeovers and LBOs were just window dressing on one of the oldest financial con games of all, the classic Ponzi or pyramid swindle. Seven Cities was colossal pyramid. Money realized from the sale of company shares was returned to the investors as dividends, which they then reinvested. The pyramid would work as long as there was a steady stream of new investors pumping in fresh cash, since nothing had been created or produced to create wealth. Inevitably the pyramid would reach a critical point, and the whole monstrous edifice of debt would come crashing down.

Yates knew well how to insulate his financial misdeeds from exposure. He worked unseen behind a mass of holding companies, dummy corporations, offshore banking accounts, and legitimate front men.

Brady Sullivan was such a front. The Columbine bank had gone belly-up because its president had illegally diverted its assets into Seven Cities holdings.

The collapse came faster than anyone would have dreamed possible, thanks to the national recession. A string of bank failures in the Midwest set off a domino effect reaching deep into the Southwest. Urgent calls were made on the Columbine's cash reserves and went unanswered. Already stung by the mismanagement of the savings and loan crisis, the government was quick to close the Columbine before it lost still more money.

Brady Sullivan was left holding the bag. Yates' role in looting the bank remained hidden. Threats of reprisals against his family if he talked had frightened Sullivan into silence, but Yates knew he couldn't rely on his silence forever. Disgrace, conviction, and a lengthy prison term were liable to loosen his tongue.

So Yates had him killed.

Tracker said, "Where do you come in?"

"Yates stole our dough, too," Mitch said. "The union's, I mean. Local 1202 of the Mining Heavy Equipment Operators and Transporters. The bastard clipped us for a couple million!"

"How'd you manage that?"

"Don't blame me. It was Honest John's fault. Honest John Brock, the union's district boss. My boss. He thought Yates was the cat's pajamas. Even sent away for his money-making course after he saw it on TV. Since there happened to be a million or two in the union pension fund just sitting there not making any money, Honest John came up with the brainstorm of putting it in Seven Cities' Double Your Money Bonds."

"So?"

"So now Yates won't give it back, the prick."

Mitch clenched and unclenched his fists. His face was red. "I get so damn mad just thinking about it," he said.

"Stealing from your outfit seems like an unhealthy proposition."

"You'd think we was the fucking Jaycees, the way he's trying to stick it to us! What does he think, that we're gonna eat it because we can't go to the cops?"

"Especially not the cops in this town."

"Boyd sold us out, sold our ass down the river. Yates paid better. Half the cops in town are on his payroll. Now that they ain't our friends no more, they're making it plenty hot for us. It's getting so a guy can't make a dishonest buck no more.

"Yates must've been planning to rip off Seven Cities right from the start. He wants all the money and he'll fight to keep it. He lives in a house up on Oldridge that's built like a bomb shelter and guarded by a private army. He's got the cops in his pocket. He's covering his ass by killing everybody who can connect him with stolen money. And he's got Killer Gordon as his number one hatchet man."

"Who's Killer Gordon?"

"Nobody knows," Mitch said, shrugging. "He's kind of a legend in this business. A mystery man. Nobody's ever seen his face and lived to tell about it. Even the guys he works for don't get to meet him. They go through some complicated rigamarole to contact him and put up the money for the contract."

"A hitman."

"More than that. An organizer, a pivot man. He's got a string of regulars that he subcontracts the big jobs out to. He plans the hit and picks the team and pays them off. They don't know who he is either, so if they get caught they can't finger him."

"This Gordon was responsible for the killing of Brady Sullivan?"

"And your pal, too," Mitch said with a sly smile. "That's just how Killer Gordon works, getting some innocent chump to do his dirty work and then chopping him so he can't talk. All wrapped up in a pretty package with nothing pointing at him."

"So you say."

"Hey, don't take my word for it, Major. Figure it out for yourself. Brady dead don't buy me nothing, it hurts me. Same with all them other guys that Gordon's been knocking off. Alive, they could've hurt Yates. But like I said, don't take my word for it. Hold Boyd's feet over a fire and see what he has to say about Killer Gordon."

"I'd like to."

"But save Maggard for me," Mitch said. "Me and him go

way back, and I'd hate like hell for somebody else to kill him first."

"I'll keep it in mind."

"Life ain't big enough for the two of us."

"That sounds final. If you'd like something of Maggard to remember him by, talk to Gene," Tracker said.

Mitch pulled a wadded handkerchief out of his pants pocket and lovingly unwrapped it to reveal the bloody tooth.

"You mean this?" he said. "I already bought it. Where do you think the squirt got that five grand to bet on you?"

"You must hate Maggard a lot to spend that much money on his tooth."

"That's the beauty part of it," Mitch said, laughing. "I didn't spend a penny! It was Sledge's dough that I owed him for his hot dog wagon that got trashed!"

"What if Sledge had won the fight?"

"Not a chance. My boy Vee was covering you the whole time. He's my top gun, a dead shot. He'd have drilled Sledge if it looked like he had you in real trouble."

"But he bet on Sledge."

"Yeah, and if he had to kill him to save you that would have meant that he won the bet."

"So no matter how you slice it, it wasn't Sledge's night."

"He wore out his welcome with me a long time back."

"You owing him money didn't improve his chances of survival," Tracker said. "Remind me not to be worth more dead than alive to you, Mitch."

"Hey, we're pals."

"Just so you don't get any wrong ideas, I'm not in this for the money."

"I never thought you were, Major."

"I'm not a cop. I'm not out to reform Mountain City's morals. I don't care who runs the rackets in this town. I've got a job to do and once it's done I'm gone and good riddance. Help me do it and you can say goodbye to Maggard and Boyd and Yates."

"Now you're talking, Major. Hot damn!"

"Gordon is a good place to start. Can't you get a line on him through your connections?"

"It was all my contacts could do to even find out he was on the case. Gordon ain't mobbed up. If he was, I could get a line on him sooner or later. But he don't go through the channels I know. He's an indie and he uses freelancers. Most times he handles it so slick that they don't even know they've pulled the job for him!"

"One last question, Mitch. If nobody knows who he is, then he could be anybody. How do you know I'm not Killer Gordon?"

Mitch stroked his chin. "Don't think I didn't think of it," he said. "But you put too much of a hurting on Yates when you barged in back at the courthouse. Now that frame-up of his is in the toilet, and the new one they hung on you won't last long. The Killer wouldn't have screwed up his own sweet setup, so you ain't him.

"Plus I did some checking on you, Major. You're a for-real flyboy who's flown the big birds. A scientist and inventor. I never heard of no hitman with his name on half-a-dozen patents, either, but maybe they do things different in your circle.

"You're a killer, Major, but you ain't Gordon."

13.

VOLLIN STUCK HIS head inside Mitch's office. "Phone," he said.

Mitch said, "Who is it?"

"I don't know. Some babe."

"What's she want?"

"She wants to talk to you. That's all Dud could get out of her. Maybe you can do better."

"If I can't do better with a babe than Dud I'll hang myself," Mitch said. "This better be good, to get me out of my chair."

He got up and went around the desk, motioning to Tracker. "Come on. I like you, Major, but not enough to leave you alone in my office. You might find my little black book," he leered.

Tracker followed him through the short passageway into the bar area. "What's that racket?" Mitch said, frowning at the noise.

It was Conner. He hadn't moved from where he sat on the floor propped up against the pool table. He was still hugging himself. His clammy face had gone from white to gray-green. He moaned louder than ever.

"He sounds constipated," Burgos said.

"I'm all busted up inside," Connor said. "I got to go to the hospital. . . ."

"The hospital, he says," Vollin said, almost smiling.

"Did you get rid of Sledge yet?"

"Porky and Concho took him out of here rolled up in a tarp. They used the pickup. They should be back in a half-hour."

"Looks like they're gonna have to make two trips," Mitch said, glancing meaningfully at Connor, who was oblivious of all but his own pain.

"This broad says it's urgent, Mitch."

"It's always urgent for the girlies when they've got a hankering for my action, Dud."

The phone was on top of the bar, and Dudley was holding the receiver. Mitch took it and leaned against the bar. "Hay-lo," he said.

"You're in great danger. They're coming to kill you," a woman said.

"Huh?"

"Run! They're coming to kill you now!"

"Who—?"

Click.

Mitch stared at the receiver in his hand.

Dudley said, "What gives?"

"I don't know if it was a gag or what. . . ."

Mitch was unhappy. That disturbed Vollin, whose hands drifted toward his guns.

Tracker had been listening in on both ends of the phone call, eavesdropping via the directional mini-mikes built into his optivisor. He thought he recognized the voice of the anonymous caller. If his recognition was right, it opened up startling new vistas of conspiracy and intrigue. But there was no time to consider the implications of that insight, not when the message itself demanded immediate action.

"Mitch?" Dudley said.

"I'm thinking."

The others were hushed, quiet, on the edge of their seats. It was so still that Mitch could hear the buzz of the electric lights, the hum of the refrigerator, the splash of water dripping from a leaky faucet, the droning dial tone of the receiver in his hand. And—something else.

Tracker said, "Listen!"

From outside came a not-so-distant rumbling, growing louder as it neared. It was coming on fast. Machine noise, sounding like an avalanche of scrap metal. Mitch dropped the phone and ran into his office. "They're coming," Vollin said, following him.

"Who?" Burgos shouted, knowing it was trouble, reaching for his gun.

Dudley ducked out of sight behind the bar, and when he reappeared thirty seconds later, he was taking guns out of a concealed storage bin and putting them on the counter. The guns, with ammo, were wrapped up inside plastic bags. They were good guns, new. There were semiautomatic pistols, big-bore revolvers, sawed-off shotguns, even a few Uzis.

The gangsters bellied up to the bar, grabbing weapons, tearing open bags. Metallic cricketing sounded as clips were fed into the guns, slides worked, rounds chambered, safeties thrown off.

Then the roaring noise outside drowned out all other sounds.

There was a false bottom in an old glass-fronted bowling trophy case in Mitch's office. Inside it was a drawer filled with weapons. Vollin grabbed two more pistols and loaded them and filled his pockets with spare clips. Mitch took out an assault rifle. It was an AR-15, the civilian version of the M-16. Unlike its military counterpart, the AR-15 could only fire in semiauto, one at a time, lacking the M-16's ability to shoot on full auto. That restriction was what allowed it to be sold to the public. But Mitch's gunsmith had filed the weapon's sear pin, a simple operation that transformed the AR-15 into a fully automatic rifle.

Mitch stuffed a home-made banana-style clip into the receiver, locking and loading it. His pocket burst at the seams with spare clips. He and Vollin exited the office, rejoining the others who were already armed to the teeth.

A truck came through the wall.

All the gangsters heard it, but Cole and Reese were the first to see it. Reese actually made the first sighting, since he was the one who was looking out of the peephole in the side door a moment before the crash. Hearing a noise, he looked through the spyhole to investigate. A truck was barreling across the parking lot, heading straight toward him. Its headlights were dark as it rushed onward. The motor was loud. It was a heavy-duty Mack-type truck, one of the city's snow emergency salt-spreading trucks, with a big V-shaped snowplow on the front and a high-walled hopper behind the cab for carrying the salt. The plow looked like the sharp-edged prow of a battleship, like the cowcatcher on an oldtime locomotive. It arrowed toward the broad side of the Palladium with irresistible momentum.

Eyes bulging, Reese stumbled back inside, pulling the door shut. He meant to run but was so eager that he tripped over his own feet.

Cole, panicked, drew his gun at the same time that the others were busily arming themselves from the weapons cache. He looked through the peephole in time to see the driver's side door open and the driver throw himself from the cab and hit the ground rolling.

The driver had bailed out in the final seconds before impact.

Cole turned to run and tripped over Reese, who had just gotten to his hands and knees. Cole fell headfirst, tangling himself up with Reese. In blind panic they kicked and punched each other as they tried to get free.

The wedge of the snowplow hit the side door like a battering ram, knocking it off its hinges so that it smashed into Reese and Cole, flattening them. The truck kept on coming through the wall, making an opening for itself as it plowed through stone and timber. It punched a hole as big as a tunnel mouth through the wall, crossed the floor, and slammed to a halt against the opposite wall, buckling it.

The collision left a boiling chaos of stones, sticks, dust, thick choking clouds of grit. For a moment it seemed that the wall of entry would completely collapse, bringing the roof down with it. A hail of bricks and beams rained down on the floor, creating man-high mounds of debris. Smoke and dust filled the space. Many of the lights blacked out, adding to the confusion.

Fresh air rushed inside through the hole in the wall. So did a band of dark-clad men with guns, killers. Killers coming to kill killers.

Pressure waves from the concussion thundered through the building. Shelves filled with bottles were ripped loose from the wall behind the bar, smashing to the floor in a squall of broken glass and booze. Dudley held on to the counter with both hands to keep from falling. Many of the gangsters were knocked down. Webs of spidery cracks opened in the walls and across the ceiling. Paint chips and plaster rained down from above, and some overhead light fixtures were torn loose from their moorings.

Then the shooting started.

Gunfire sleeted out of the smoke clouds billowing into the bar, a spray of steel ripping through the space at waist-height. Those who were on their feet were cut down. There was the sound of bullets pulping flesh, the jackhammer reports of automatic weapons fire.

Red, his pool-playing partner, and the kibitzer made a threesome in death. They were all standing grouped together between the pool tables, their forms shadowy outlines in the smoke and dust. As the slugs ripped them, they ran backward until they bounced against the wall. The wall held them up while they were shot to pieces. Arms outspread, they jogged in place until the shooting stopped, then fell down dead together at the same time, like the finale to a precision dance team's routine.

The kibitzer flopped face down on the floorboards an arm's length from Tracker, who lay prone behind the cover of the corner of the bar. The corpse was red, ragged, and sieved.

The enemy fire came from the opposite direction, from attacking gunmen spread out in a loose line across the foot of the lanes, taking cover behind the curved benches and tables of the bowlers' pits. Lances of fire flashed from the muzzles of twenty guns. The fusillade rose in fury as the attackers concentrated their fire. Bullets tore through booths, spraying splinters. Lines of bullet holes cratered the walls, kicking up a ghostly white mist of powdered plaster.

The murky haze was crystal-clear to Tracker, thanks to his video optics. Infrared imaging pinpointed the location of each foe by the undisguisable thermal signature of his body heat. Not even hiding behind cover could blind Tracker's heat-seeking sensors. The attckers appeared as an even dozen man-shaped glowing blobs of light, scattered high and low in a loose arc facing the setback bar area.

Tracker had a gun, an Uzi he'd taken off the counter and armed before any of Mitch's crowd could stop him. He had two spare clips, too. He waited, biding his time. The enemy fire had reached its crescendo, a symphonic chorus of ballistic clangor, a percussion suite in a tin factory. It was the covering fire. Then the rushers would make their move.

Silence slammed down as the shooting stopped. Debris dropped from above. Brass cartridges spilled on waxed wooden floorboards.

The first rushers came in two teams of two. They charged up the opposite ends of the wide, shallow three-step stairway to the bar.

Tracker targeted the two-man team nearest him. The first man cleared the way with a riot shotgun, pumping big roaring blasts into furniture and bodies. Smoke and dust must have confused him, or maybe he was just squirrelly, because he blew away the juke box and banged big holes into the dead bodies of Red and his two pals. The second man covered the first. He was armed with a high-powered hunting rifle. Wary, crouched low, he held his fire, waiting for a target he could see. This team advanced, using the bar for cover. The other team made its approach shielded by the back of the row of booths.

A big shard of glass from the shattered wall-mounted mirror fell to the floor. The shot-gunner wheeled his weapon into line and triggered a blast into the side of the bar. The cagey rifleman continued to hold fire. He had good control, hence was dangerous. Tracker shot him first.

Tracker held the advantage because he could see clearly where the attackers were half-blinded by smoke, dust, airborne grit. The battering truck had opened the way for them, but had also created the chaos that now handicapped them.

From a prone two-handed firing position, Tracker lifted the muzzle of the Uzi, aligning it with the rifleman. This fractional movement was caught by the other, who instantly went into action. He held the rifle in two hands, at waist-height, finger near the trigger. He only had to move the rifle barrel an inch down to nail Tracker, but it might as well have been a mile.

Tracker acted while the other reacted, squeezing a three-shot burst into the middle of the rifleman's chest. The rifleman backflipped, dead.

The upper half of the jukebox was a smorgasbord of pulverized glass, plastic, chrome strips, and smoldering lumps of fused vinyl. The shot-gunner tried to duck back behind the cover of its solid metal base, but he didn't get his trailing leg out of the line of fire in time. Tracker stitched it with a three-shot burst. The shot-gunner screamed. Tracker nailed him with another quick burst, again spraying the leg. High-powered slugs inflicted terrible damage on flesh and blood and bone. The wounded leg looked like roadkill.

Convulsively the shot-gunner jerked the trigger, firing a blast straight up into the ceiling. It hit a long tube light in a tin shade hanging from the ceiling on two chains. One chain was blasted loose from its fastenings on the ceiling. The fixture dropped, still anchored to a chain at one end. It swung down toward the wall like a pendulum, crashing into the shotgunner. The shotgunner slammed into the wall, bounced off, and fell beyond the jukebox. Sprawled on the floor, he glimpsed Tracker's face an instant before a blast from the Uzi obliterated his own.

Tracker rolled behind the cover of the bar before the return fire peppered the general area. He lay so flat that he could feel the grain of the floorboards pressing into his face.

Plenty of gunfire probed in his direction, more than the other two-man team could put out by themselves, although they were doing their damnedest to nail him. One was armed with an assault rifle, hosing the corner of the L-shaped bar. The other cradled a machine pistol whose muzzle belched fire as it barked and stuttered. Other guns joined the chorus, homing in on Tracker. Tracker thanked his lucky stars that the bar was stoutly made of thick wood. Even with all that firepower arrayed against him, it would be a long time before the barricade was shot away. From where he lay he could see under the swinging half-door at his end of the bar. Dudley lay sprawled flat with the bottoms of his shoes facing Tracker and one arm stretched out in front of him. He wasn't moving. Tracker couldn't tell if he was alive or dead.

The attackers massed for their big rush. Tracker wasn't shooting back, emboldening some of them to rise in a half-crouch and warily advance. The surviving pair of rushers stood side by side, backs to the row of booths, advancing sideways in a crablike motion with their weapons firing alternate bursts into Tracker's corner.

They were the easiest shots Vee Vollin ever made. He was crouching in the corner behind an overturned table in the next to last booth. His back was curved, his legs were folded with the knees close to his chin, and he held a flat blue-black .45 in each hand. Both men had their backs to him. The one with the machine pistol had a ponytail and wore a long dark raincoat. The one with the assault rifle had slicked-back, lead-colored hair, was heavyset, and wore a green and black–checked hunting jacket and a leather cap with furry earflaps worn pinned-up.

Vollin didn't take chances on their wearing flak jackets or

bulletproof vests. He shot them both in the back of the head, one shot each. With a .45, one is enough. He didn't try any fancy trick shooting with two guns at once, just squeezed off a quick two with the gun in his left hand.

Shots blasted in his vicinity but didn't do more than discomfort him since the invaders weren't sure where the firing had come from that killed the duo.

Dudley moved. He wasn't dead. His limbs shook like a dog having a bad dream. He groaned, stirred. As he rolled on his side, a raw red hole in the back of his left shoulder showed that he'd been hit. He'd been lying on top of a weapon, an assault rifle with an attached grenade launcher complete with bulb-shaped grenade. He dragged his legs under him and sat up with his back against the stainless steel bins under the contour. His bow tie was turned sideways. So was his face, which was twisted from the strain. He cradled the grenade launcher in his arms, hugging it to keep from dropping it because of his shakes.

The invaders rallied for the final assault. Already they'd sustained more casualties than they'd reckoned on. They weren't soldiers, disciplined to fight as a unit. They were a gang of killers banded together to do a job, not fight a war. The intended victims weren't supposed to be hitting back this hard.

"Let's finish this fast! We ain't got all night!" That was the voice of one of them, possibly the leader, a voice unknown to Tracker. He was smart enough not to show himself as a target. "One last rush will finish them," he said. "We'll overwhelm 'em with firepower and numbers, just swat 'em down!"

Before they could lay down a barrage of gunfire to cover their rush, Dudley shakily rose to his feet, leaning against the bar for support. One of the invaders recognized the grenade launcher and said, "Holy shit!" The weapon see-sawed up and down in Dudley's shaky hands.

Somebody shot at him, missed. "Don't hit the grenade, you'll blow us all up!" the leader shrieked.

Another shot rang out, goosing a wordless shriek from the leader. A rifle bullet, fired by an expert. It took Dudley square in the middle of the throat, knocking him down.

"Damn your eyes, Nichols!" the leader shouted.

"What're you hollering for? I got him, didn't I?"

"You could have blasted us sky-high if you missed, you idiot!"

"Well, I didn't," Nichols said smugly. "I never miss."

"Let's kill their asses before they come up with something else!" another voice said.

"Don't lose your guts," the leader said. "Looks like there's only two of them, and one's just got a pistol from the sound of it."

"Watch out for that fucking machine-gun," somebody said.

"Hey, you! We gone kill you all, y'hear!" twanged a voice with a sharp nasal edge.

"Shut up, Otis," the leader said.

"Sure, Dwight."

"Shut up and start shooting—*Look out!*"

The leader's panic was induced by a square flat object that came hurtling from behind the back of the bar, pinwheeling through the air. "Shoot, shoot!" Dwight shouted.

Nichols was already in motion, firing his rifle from the hip, blasting the skimmer in midair as if he were shooting skeet. What he had shot was the swinging half-door at the back of the bar, which Tracker had ripped off its hinges and sailed up and out to create a diversion. It worked. He dove headfirst through the entryway behind the bar.

Nichols, fast, saw the flicker of movement and fired too late.

"Behind the bar! Shoot, shoot!" Dwight said.

There was shooting, lots of it. It tore into the side of the bar and the wall behind the top of it, but not into Tracker.

Dudley's eyes flicked open as Tracker took the grenade launcher from what he'd thought were dead hands. Dudley tried to say something, but the effort only made the blood bubble out of the hole in his throat.

Otis tried to storm the bar like a movie marine taking a machine-gun nest. He was a cowboy with a pair of pearl-handled, chrome-plated, short-barreled .38s, one in each hand. "Only one way to get that honker!" he shouted, rushing the bar with both guns blazing.

Vollin had two guns, too, but he only needed one to handle Otis. He put one blazing slug in the middle of Otis' wide strong back.

Otis lurched forward in mid-stride as if he'd been hit in the spine with a pickaxe. His back bowed forward and his arms stuck out from his sides.

"Otis! Goddamn you—*Otis!*" Nichols was the one shouting Otis' name but he was careful not to show himself.

Otis stumbled forward, running out of steam. His knees folded right about when he neared the bar stools. Falling, he grabbed the seat of one with both hands and held on with his knees on the floor. Light glinted off one of his guns, catching his eye. He shook his head, as if to clear it. Remembering he'd been shot, he looked over his shoulder in the direction from which the bullet had come. Seeing Vollin, he tried to untangle his hands, freeing his guns. He glanced back over his shoulder, and Vollin shot him in the eye.

"Otis!"

Bullets ripped through partitions separating the booths, but they had a long way to go to reach Vollin, and none of them made it the distance.

"Quit wasting your fire and cover the bar," Nichols said to the rest of them, all icy business. "Get the one behind the bar first, and we can pick off the other one later."

"That's good sense, Nichols," Dwight said.

"That poor dead boy's momma is my kid sister. I'm the one who's got to tell her that he's dead—dead at twenty-two, before he ever lived."

"We'll get the bastards, Nichols, I promise you that—"

Mitch popped out from where he'd been hiding in the small passageway between the bar area and his office.

The invaders attention was focused mainly on Tracker when Mitch cut loose with the AR-15. A group of about four or five of them were grouped at the opposite corner, guns at the ready to blast Tracker the instant he showed himself. Two of the group were over to one side by themselves, angling to line up a shot on Vollin. All five were meat for Mitch's grinder. His technique was crude but effective. He just held down the trigger, emptying the clip on auto fire, spraying lead as if he were working a fire hose. He was strong, a bull, and he was able to hold the rifle rock steady against the recoil of uninterrupted fire.

Some of the five shouted in dismay, some were silent, all were extinct within a few seconds.

Mitch whipped the lead stream to the side, seeking the larger group of nine, over by the end of the row of booths. Most of them managed to scramble to safety in time, including Nichols and the leader. One was winged but managed to stumble out of range. The other had his legs cut out from under him and fell forward on his face, losing his gun, which skittered away from him. He dragged himself forward by his hands, like a bug whose lower half has been squashed. Mitch tried to finish him off but his gun clicked on empty. The barrel glowed a hot dull red, smoke curling from it. Mitch ducked back into the passageway, out of the line of fire. Tracker popped up and fired the grenade launcher. There was a percussive springlike sound as the grenade was launched and armed. Tracker aimed it to hit the ceiling behind the invaders. He ducked back below the bar in the same breath, covering his ears with his hands and opening his mouth wide for protection against the concussion. He didn't see the bulb-shaped grenade bank off the ceiling above the lanes like a well-angled pool shot. The grenade bounced off the ceiling tiles and fell clattering and spinning in the middle of lane number eight.

A fragmentation grenade. The explosion transformed it to a storm of white-hot steel shards moving at supersonic speeds. Those in the blast area were minced as thoroughly as if they'd been thrown into a food processor. The ones at the edges of the blast were less fortunate. They lived to experience the numbing horror of their own mangled bodies. But not for long. Even before the dust had settled and the smoke cleared, the winners delivered the *coup de grâce*.

14.

MITCH FED A regular 15-shot clip into the rifle, only half the number of rounds which the banana clip had contained. To make up the difference in lost firepower, he toted a double-barreled sawed-off shotgun. Assault rifle in one hand and sawed-off shotgun in the other, he came out to lead off the clean-up.

Vollin rose and came pouring out of the booth like liquid smoke, falling into step beside Mitch.

The invader who'd dropped with dead legs was still alive. He looked up fearfully as the mobster and his hatchet man approached. Whimpering, he drew a breath to plead for mercy. Vollin shot him, drilling him to the floor. He didn't bat an eye as he stepped over the corpse.

The bomb blast site was a hell pit. Hundreds of fist-sized craters pocked the walls, floors, the wheel-shaped reservoir for holding returned bowling balls. A hole ringed by black scorch marks was blasted through the dropped ceiling. Many small fires smoldered where white-hot steel had ignited wood.

As for the invaders who'd caught the full fury of the blast, their sprawling forms looked like mounds of barbecued meat that had been run through a threshing machine. A few of them were still moving, twitcing, mewling, jerking. Vollin finished them off, firing off-handedly, not seeming to take aim, just pointing the gun like a finger and firing. But each shot hit its mark, bringing instant death as it bored through a living brain.

"Hey, look at this," Mitch said.

Vollin focused on the object of Mitch's interest, a seared and blackened body curled into the curve of a bench. Mitch put his foot on its shoulder, rolling the body over on its back. Some fluke of the explosion had left the body untouched above the shoulders, with even the head hairs surviving unsinged. Below the shoulders, the body resembled a crushed can of tomato paste. "Fucking Nichols," Mitch said. "How about that?"

"That explains a lot of things," Vollin said. "He's alive."

"No way."

"I saw him move his eyes, now he's playing possum."

Mitch stepped down hard on Nichols' chest. Nichols' eyes snapped open as he groaned aloud in agony. "Nichols, you fucking prick, you tried to kill me," Mitch said.

Nichols hissed up at him, blood bubbling through clenched teeth.

"Nichols, this is Vollin, Vee Vollin. Hear me good. My cousin Oscar from Slickrock has been fucking your wife for the last five years. He's been putting it to her in your own bed every time you've been away on one of your hunting trips."

Nichols' face contorted like invisible fish hooks were pulling it in several different directions at once.

"Wonder if he's laying up with her right now?" Mitch said. "Think about that on your way to hell." Mitch took his foot off Nichols' chest.

"I was looking that big hick Otis in the eye when I shot it out," Vollin said.

Nichols thrashed for a few seconds before Mitch emptied one of the shotgun barrels in his face. "Nichols used to be one of my hunting buddies, he was a guest in my house plenty of times, faw crissakes, and then he goes and tries to kill me, the prick!"

"The sharks smell blood, Mitch."

"Yeah—their own."

Brrrrrrrrrriiiiiiiip!

Mitch and Vollin both started like they were trying to jump out of their skins when they were surprised by the unexpected chatter of gunfire behind them. They spun, guns ready, only to see Dwight a half-dozen paces behind them with a gun in his hand. He'd been caught rising out of his hiding place behind some benches, and the bullets caught him while he was still in a half-crouch. Dwight shivered like he was stuck in an ice-cold shower. The gunfire stopped and so did he, dead.

Tracker had done the shooting. He stood leaning over the near edge of the bar, where he had used the countertop as a firing platform to steady the Uzi when he burned Dwight down. "He must have gone to cover right before the blast. I kept a low profile just in case anybody was playing possum," Tracker said.

"Having you around is paying off already," Mitch said.

Vollin was miffed at having to share the spotlight with another gun. He went to look at Dwight. "It's feuding time now," he said.

Tracker came out from behind the bar, nimbly scrambling over the top, touching down lightly on the other side.

"You just bagged yourself a Scroggins, Major," Mitch said.

"What's a Scroggins?"

"That is," Mitch said, pointing at Dwight. "So's most of the other stiffs, unless I miss my guess. Not counting my guys, that is. Scroggins are trash. They live in the back hills of the Kettle, a whole clan of them got a settlement up on a ridge. They're so inbred, with cousins marrying cousins all the time, that half of them got webbed fingers and feet, and one out of every four of them is born brain-dead. And those are the good ones. There's a lot of them, and they stick together, and as long as they mind their own business, it ain't worth tangling with them, because if you get in a scrap with one, you can't rest until you've wiped out every last one of them."

"Looks like they've stopped minding their business and started minding yours."

"Yeah, and I'll tell you why. My good buddy—and yours—Sgt. Maggard is married into the clan. Dwight here is his brother-in-law. Was."

"You and Maggard should really get along good now that you've iced Dwight," said Vollin to Tracker with smiling malice.

"I don't think the sarge is going to be around long enough for our friendship to ripen," Tracker said.

"Not when I catch up with him," Mitch said. "I'll shoot his guts out, then I'll make it a point to wipe out them baby-raping Scroggins scum. I should have cleaned up them mountain misfits a long time ago!"

"Maybe we should try getting out of here alive first, Mitch."

"Not a bad idea, Vee," Mitch said after a pause.

"Don't shoot!"

A passageway stretched between the far end of the bar and the wall, leading into a tiny kitchen with metal-topped counters and a blackened grill that hadn't been cleaned since Carter was president. The sooty cubicle stank of stale grease.

"It's me—Gene! Don't shoot, I'm coming out!"

Gene came crawling out of the dark closet-like space on his hands and knees. When he rounded the corner, coming into view of the others, he stood on his knees and raised his hands to show they were empty. Eyes wide, he took in the scene of violent death and destruction.

"This guy's got more lives than a cat," Mitch said to nobody in particular. To Gene, he said, "Get up, faw crissakes, you look ridiculous."

The little man with the dour mustache rose, shoulders hunched as if in anticipation of a blow. "Jeeze, some party," he said, trying to brazen it out. Tracker liked him all the better for the attempt.

"You sat out the fight in the kitchen and now you show yourself when the fighting's over and it's safe to come out."

"Can you think of a better time? I'm no gunman, Mitch. Anyhow," he said, looking over his shoulder toward the kitchen, "I'm not the only one who sat out the fight."

"Huh?"

"There's somebody else in there, Mitch," Vollin said, covering the kitchen with his guns.

"Come out of there, you," he said. Burgos slunk out, shamefaced.

"Why, you dirty rotten son of a bitch," Mitch said. He put his weapons down on the bar and bore down on Burgos. He was barehanded, Burgos held a handgun at his side pointing down. Ignoring the gun, Mitch charged.

"Don't—"

Mitch stepped on Burgos' toes, kicked him in the shins, grabbed his tie, and pulled his head down. Then he rocked him with a back-handed right across the chops. Burgos' head swiveled to the side from the impact. Mitch smacked him on that side, knocking the head back the other way. Mitch did that for a while, working out on the other's face like a boxer hitting a speed bag. Burgos took it, the gun in his hand forgotten. He sank to his knees when Mitch finally let go of his shirtfront. "Yellow punk," Mitch said. "You've been leeching around on the payroll for months and you turn to shit as soon as the shooting starts!"

"Don't kill me, Mitch! Please!"

"You've got it coming."

"Please, Mitch, don't!"

Tracker was alive with intentness, as if listening to messages only he could hear. That was the impression he made on the others who little dreamed how right they were. Tracker was monitoring a burst of radio traffic on the city police net. Radio silence had prevailed up to and throughout the death squad's assault, denying Tracker advance notice of the attack. The police band was active now, cross-cut with quick commands and responses from a number of units in the field. They were closing in on the Palladium.

"No time for that now, Mitch."

"The hell you say, Major. I'll make time to kick the stomach clean out of this yellowbelly!"

"Big trouble's on the way, police and lots of them."

"What are you, a bird dog?" Vollin said.

"Listen to him, he knows what he's saying! Shades has got a kind of a sixth sense about cops or something," Gene said.

Mitch changed gears. "I ain't gonna kill you after all, Burgos."

"Thanks, Mitch, oh thank the Virgin—"

"That is, I ain't gonna kill you unless you're still here by the time I get done counting to ten."

"Mitch, wait, please—"

"One, two, three—"

"Mitch!" Burgos shrieked.

"Five, six, sev—"

Burgos was up and running, the gun still in one hand. He had to step lively to keep from tripping over corpses and debris. He was stampeded into full panicked flight.

He turned left, disappearing into the darkness pooled at the front of the building. The big glass double doors at the main entrance were boarded over, but light from the streetlamps on Rowe Street shone through cracks and gaps where the plywood sheets had been imperfectly joined. There was enough light to see by.

The barrier wasn't as impassable as it seemed to be from the outside. Thick crossbeams were laid across the tops of the twin handgrips where each set of double doors came together, effectively barring them. Burgos went to the second set of doors from the left and tugged at the crossbeam.

He wrestled the glass doors open. Two sheets of plywood, eight feet tall, overlapped in front of the doors. The nails joining them had been loosened. Burgos shouldered the plywood hard, nails squealing as they tore free. The plywood sheets came apart at the bottom but stayed together on top. From the waist down, the sheets were pried open about three feet apart. Night air rushed through the gap, fanning Burgos' overheated face. Crouching low, Burgos held the outer flap open with his free hand while he tried to worm through. Outside, it was still and dark. A line of jutting nails ripped open the shoulder and sleeve of Burgos' jacket as he bulled his way through. He crawled into the open air. He knelt on the wide white concrete top step of the front stairway. The plywood sheets flapped closed behind him. He still had the gun in his hands. He restrained the urge to throw it as far away as he could. If he got out of this, he vowed to turn over a new leaf, get reformed. He'd give up guns and violence for good, clean up his act and get into a smooth racket where he could make an easy buck, far from the world of kill or be killed.

Lights flashed on. Spotlights blazed full into his face, dazzling his eyes, near-blinding in their intensity. The Palladium's front was bathed in harsh white light, like a stage set when the curtain rises. Burgos stood on his knees, whimpering. He raised an arm to shield his eyes from the punishing glare. Behind him, multiple shadows cast by the lights moved their arms, fluttering across the screenlike backdrop of the boarded-up front.

Two cars were parked nose to nose with their sides facing the front of the building. Both big dark Ford sedans, definitely unmarked police cars. The searchlights were mounted on the cars and trained on him. Armed men huddled behind the improvised barricade, pointing guns at him.

Burgos was too light-blinded to notice that one of the ambushers resembled a living mummy from the neck up, thanks to a head wrapped in bandages. A black-visored uniform cap was perched on top of his head, and he wore a patrolman's blue tunic unbuttoned down the middle and minus the badge.

It was Maggard and he, too, had a gun pointed at Burgos. He

took a deep breath to give the order to fire, but the effort sent waves of agony churning through the dreamy haze of narcotizing painkillers that enabled him stand the pain and keep going.

The others in his special squad held their fire, waiting to take their cue from the sergeant.

"What's the stall? You waiting for him to sing a couple choruses of 'Mammy' or something?"

Detective Monty's sarcasm was the first thing that Maggard heard as his pain diminished. It acted like a dentist's drill on the exposed nerve of his hurting head. Maggard shot at Burgos. Tears of pain and the discomfort of a bandaged head made him miss, but not by much.

"Stop! Don't shoot, I give up!"

Maggard put a bullet into Burgos before he could think of throwing down his gun. The slug hit Burgos in the middle. He felt like he'd been run through by a flagpole.

The others opened fire. Burgos crumpled, fell on his side, and rolled over on his back, dead eyes turned skyward.

"Who was that?" said one of the squad when the shooting stopped.

"You ask too many questions," Monty said.

Those still inside the Palladium didn't need Tracker's formidable array of listening devices to hear Burgos' finish. Gunfire crashed like a salute from a firing squad.

Burgos was silenced in mid-scream. Bullets ventilated the plywood panels, disintegrating the glass doors behind them, tearing up the front lobby.

Mitch was watching from a side window out of the line of fire. The glass was painted black, except for a clear section as big as a man's palm in the lower right hand corner. Mitch watched through that. When the shooting stopped, he said, "Burgos earned his pay after all."

"I call that making it the hard way," Tracker said.

"It's Maggard's Specials, the goon squad. They must be the back-up in case the Scroggins fucked up. Probably got all the exits covered."

"We'll have to shoot our way out of here," Vollin said.

"There's a better way," Tracker said.

"Scared to shoot it out with the cops?"

"Why shoot when you can ride?"

"I don't get you," Mitch said.

"The truck doesn't look too badly damaged. If it starts, we can ride it out of here."

"Sure, it'll be in great shape after crashing through a wall," Vollin said.

"The plow took most of the impact. Those trucks are built tough."

"We better do something," Gene fretted. "From the sound of those sirens, the rest of the cops will be here any second."

"Who asked you?" Mitch said.

"I was just trying to help."

"You want to help, pick up a gun and start shooting."

Gene swallowed hard. "You know I'm no gunman, Mitch."

"Shaddup, then."

Tracker knew that the truck was in pretty good shape, since he'd screened it in the infrared mode and found no obvious defects that would prevent it from running. He turned and started toward it. Mitch said, "Hey, where are you going?"

"Stay here if you like. I'm leaving."

"Wait for me, Shades!" Gene trotted after Tracker's heels like a faithful dog. After a brief pause, Mitch shrugged and followed, with a skeptical Vollin in tow.

Dust clouds still roiled and churned around the truck, helping to hide Tracker and the others from the gunmen stationed outside to cover the hole in the wall so it couldn't be used for an exit. Fresh air poured in through the hole, but not fast enough to clear away the murk.

The truck motor had stalled from the crash. The engine block and massive drive shaft were intact. Tracker could see them through the solid metal body with his infrared vision. Some fluids were leaking from the engine but not enough to put it out of commission. It wouldn't go far before breaking down completely, but it would be all right in the short term—if it could be started.

The snow plow had accordioned with the tip buried in the wall. The girder-like front bumper was bent at odd angles, the radiator grille was caved in, the hood was popped open, and the windshield was frosted with cracks. But the tires and wheel axles were intact.

"Lemme try," Mitch said, climbing into the cab behind the steering wheel. "I used to drive a rig like this back when I had to work for a living."

While Mitch played around with the controls, the others kept behind the truck for cover. Mitch tried to start it a few times but nothing happened.

Shots were fired into the building through the hole in the wall. Only a few of them, and they all splashed harmlessly against the bricks. "They're getting the range," Tracker said.

"How about it, Mitch?"

"Don't bug me, Vee, I got to concentrate." Mitch did some more fiddling with the starter, choke, and gas pedal. The engine coughed, lurched, hammered a few piston strokes, then quit. "Fuck!" Mitch banged his hand against the steering wheel, cracking it. Those outside began shooting in earnest.

Muttering obscenities nonstop, Mitch labored over the controls. The motor ripped out a series of noises, shuddered, then boomed some backfires that sounded like mortar shells going off.

The police shooting stopped.

"They probably think we got a cannon in here or something," Gene joked nervously.

Vee said, "Mitch!"

Not looking up, Mitch opened his mouth to bark an obscenity that was never delivered. The motor roared into life, spewing a mass of black smoke out the stacks. The truck shivered with vibrations. The engine ran as roughly as it could without shaking itself apart, but it was running. Mitch nursed it along, carefully feeding it more fuel to keep from flooding it as it revved up.

The police resumed shooting at full blast.

Vollin used his gun butt to smash out the frosted windshield, scattering crystal cubes of safety glass everywhere. "I like to see who I'm shooting at," he said.

The cab was big but four was a crowd. Mitch was at the wheel, Vollin was in the middle, and Tracker sat on the passenger's side. Gene was forced to crouch in a ball in the well under the dashboard and instrument panel.

Mitch said, "What the hell, you ain't shooting."

"I don't mind, I'm safer down here!" Gene said.

Bullets spanged against the back of the truck, deflected by the solid metal hopper. Tracker said, "If one of those should hit a tire—"

"Don't worry, we was just leaving," Mitch said. "I hope. Well, here goes nothing." He wrestled the stick into gear. Reverse gave good traction and they needed it because the tip of the snow plow was planted pretty solidly in the wall. Mitch hit it too hard the first time and the truck nearly stalled, scaring him. He was more careful on the next attempt, deliberately feeding it fuel as he piled up RPMs.

The invisible tug of war ended suddenly as the wall yielded up its prize. The instant release of tension when the plow was pulled free sent the truck zooming backward. It was almost to the hole in the opposite wall when Mitch finally recovered control.

The wall that had been speared now began to buckle, rippling like a curtain in a breeze. A thing made of stone and steel, plaster and wood should not fold like cloth.

A rift opened in clouds of dust, letting Tracker see the scene outside the hole in the wall reflected in the truck's side-mounted rearview mirror. Beyond the police barricade, a line of flashing blue and red lights spanned the horizon in both directions as far as the eye could see. They were the lights of a fleet of police cars charging toward the Palladium. Less than a quarter-mile away, and closing fast.

Being rammed by the truck had fatally weakened the wall. The top of it started to tear loose where the roof joined it. A seam opened in the wall from ceiling to floor. A rafter beam ripped free at one end and started banging against the wall. Pieces of roofing material as big as serving platters pelted the truck. Vollin said, "The whole place is coming down!"

"And me with no insurance," Mitch said, cursing as he threw the truck into forward gear. He whipped the steering wheel hard left, turning the truck in the same direction, so that it faced the front of the building.

Vollin said, "Mitch—"

Mitch turned on the headlights, but the dust clouds were so thick that the lights actually lessened visibility. The fog lights worked better, thrusting low pale beams deep into the murk.

"Hold on tight," Mitch said, stomping the gas petal, blackening the diesel smoke pouring out of the stacks. The truck bounced along the aisle behind the back of the lanes, bulling toward the front of the building, flattening any obstacles in its path.

"Mitch!" Vollin's shout was lost in the roar of the motor and the grinding rumble of the building coming apart around them.

A set of glass doors stood between the vestibule and the front lobby. The truck shouldered it aside as if the thick panes of safety glass were made of spun sugar. The top of the portal was about two feet too low for the truck to clear it. No problem. The truck widened the space on its way out. The nose dipped as the vehicle slanted down a short stairway. Tracker had to hold tight to keep from being bounced headfirst into the cab roof.

The rest of the vestibule was little longer than the truck itself. The boarded-up front entrance seemed to hurtle forward on a collision course. Plywood paneling braced with beams and planks proved only slightly more resistant than glass doors. With a splintering crash the wooden panels exploded as if struck by a wrecker's ball.

Maggard's special squad started firing.

Tracker didn't like to fight cops, but any resemblance between Maggard's men and real police officers was strictly coincidental. He opened up with the Uzi, strafing the two-car barricade.

Vollin gripped the top of the instrument panel for support with one hand and fired his pistol with the other.

The front wheels went over a bump—Burgos. So did the back wheels. The truck tilted, shuddering down the front stone steps. The battered snowplow made an unholy racket, striking sparks as it hit the hardtop pavement of the parking lot. The shocks and springs were good but they had to work to absorb the strain. A little harder, and the truck would have smashed its drive shaft against the asphalt.

Bullets bounced off the plow, holed the front fenders.

Mitch steered straight for the two-car barricade. Hunched low over the wheel to present a smaller target for police bullets, he licked his lips and grinned big. "I been itching to settle some scores with these lousy cops," he said.

They weren't shooting anymore, they were running, scrambling to get clear of the onrushing truck. Maggard ran as fast as anyone. Tracker recognized him because he was the only one there who looked like the Mummy in cop drag, due to the bandages from his injuries. Maggard might have made it, if not for Vee Vollin's deadly guns. Vollin burned him down with .45 lead.

Mitch aligned the snowplow's leading edge with the place

where the two unmarked cars touched nose to nose, then increased speed.

Collision!

A hurtling juggernaut, the truck plowed into the two cars and tossed them aside. The car on the left overturned and skidded on its back, the one on the right pinwheeled end over end before crashing and burning. The truck wobbled, fishtailing while Mitch fought for control. He straightened out its course but the vehicle still wobbled. The engine made a funny new noise, and a feathery plume of steam vented from somewhere in its guts. "Still going, though," Mitch said.

He crossed the lot, hopped the curb, and drove into a cross street that intersected Rowe at right angles.

Before the cops staked out around the Palladium could catch their breath, the building collapsed. A long wall fell outward and the roof fell in, bringing down the other long wall with it. A column of smoke and dust rose into the overcast night sky.

A police car rounded the corner, entering the street. It came from the south, but the long line of police cars was coming down from the city north of Redrow.

Mitch headed for Rowe Street. The newly arrived police car lay ahead, coming toward him. It swerved to avoid a head-on crash, but Mitch swung the truck far to one side to hit it. He clipped the police car's front, disabling it so it couldn't follow.

The truck cut across Rowe, oblivious to the two-way traffic. Police cars only used the street, closing in from both ends. The truck went south along a street on the other side of Rowe, entering the old industrial district. Mountains of masonry loomed on either side, the crumbling hulks of long-abandoned factories, warehouses, machine yards. Only the squares had street lamps, and most of them were dark; the long blocks between them were thick with black darkness. Mitch switched off the fog lights, blacking out the truck. There was enough light to see by.

Redrow was in a valley. Rowe Street ran across the bottom of it. South of Rowe, the land began to rise again, climbing to the far side of the valley.

Two police cars followed in pursuit, others raced up the roads bracketing the trucks escape route. More flocked to the scene by the minute.

Tracker and Vollin reloaded their weapons. A spent clip fell to the floor near Gene, who was still stuffed under the padded dashboard. "Owww, my head," he complained. "Hey, what's going on up there?" Nobody answered him.

"There's woods at the top of the hill, lots of them," Mitch said. "Once I reach it, there ain't a cop alive I can't lose!"

The slope steepened as they neared the top. The engine was working harder than ever but the truck still slowed. Its speed dropped to ten miles per hour when it began the last long block before the summit. All but a few of the police cars were still at the bottom of the hill, but of those few the nearest was two hundred feet from the truck and climbing fast.

A blue light flashed on top of the hill. Mitch said, "What's that?"

"More cops, probably. Just one, it looks like," Vollin said.

"We'll blast our way through!"

Distortions flickered across Tracker's view screens, vanishing almost immediately as the circuitry automatically adjusted to the new source of interference. The blue light glowed brighter, like a tiny blue sun.

The engine spasmed, throwing a fit. The illuminated instrument panel dimmed its lights. The truck's forward motion was virtually nil. "We ain't gonna make it," Gene said.

But the handful of police cars close behind were affected, too. They slowed, their lights fading, sirens fading.

The blue light glowed brighter by contrast to the deepening darkness. "What is this, a gag?" Mitch said.

"It's no gag," Tracker said. "Listen to me: if that blue light comes at us, shoot it."

"Huh?"

"Hit it with everything you've got. It's a weapon. I can't explain now, but trust me, hit it with everything you've got. Enough bullets might short-circuit it."

"You're nuts!" Vollin said.

15.

The truck slipped, then started to roll backward, pulled by gravity. Mitch bailed out on the driver's side. Vollin, incredibly quick, wriggled out the space where the windshield had been, scuttled across the hood on hands and feet, and dove over the side. Tracker grabbed Gene by the scruff of the neck and hauled him out from under the dashboard, taking him with him as he abandoned the cab.

The police cars were slipping backward, too. They were dead and dark. The other cars far below couldn't seem to creep higher than the middle of the hill; their lights were pale puny things. The street lights were dead clear down to Rowe Street.

The blue globe lifted, a high arching comet, then suddenly plunged downward.

Five front-running police cars, far ahead of the rest of the pack, had failed when they were within a hundred feet of their quarry. Now, the drivers wrestled with vehicles gone powerless, rolling backward out of control, gathering speed with every second. Boyd and Monty were in one of those cars, along with two uniformed cops. Boyd had picked up Monty after the special squad was routed. Boyd had crowded the truck, pushing his souped-up car to third in line of the pursuit vehicles. Then the power went out.

Boyd heaved at a wheel made balky by the loss of power steering. The radio vomited an ear-splitting torrent of white noise, the only piece of hardware that was even semi-functioning.

Boyd was pissed. The whole sweet setup had gone inexplicably sour, starting with the botched courthouse killings. Maggard's injuries rendered him all but useless just when he was needed the most. Now he was dead. Yates was mad and scared, in about equal proportions. They'd gotten a break when a patrol car ran a routine check on a pickup and wound up nabbing Porky and Concho for carting Sledge's corpse. They were tough; it took the special squad's skilled interrogators a full five minutes to make them confess all.

Leery of tangling with Mitch head-on, Boyd had set the Scroggins clan on him. They had been supplied with plenty of guns and ammo and a city snowplow truck that wouldn't be reported stolen until twenty-four hours later. The job had been too big for them and they'd blown it, getting themselves killed in the bargain. Small loss there. Then Maggard's goon squad had been scattered like tenpins by the hijacked truck. The Palladium's destruction was going to take some tall explaining. And if Mitch should somehow escape to fight another day, disaster!

But Mitch wouldn't escape, not when Boyd and four other cars were so close they could almost reach out and shoot him—

The blue light came, the cars stalled, and the collisions began.

At first they were just mild fender-benders, mere love taps delivered at a few miles per hour as the clustered police cars curved backward into each other, impacting at odd angles. But the whole mass was also moving downhill, and as the collisions multiplied, the damage worsened. The mad, frustrated cops shouted at each other in vain, unable to halt the chain reaction of crunching metal and breaking glass.

Then came the fireball.

The blue globe dropped into the hopper of the truck. A blinding blue flash was followed by a shattering explosion.

Tracker lay face down on a patch of ground on the right side of the street, as far from the truck as he'd been able to get before it blew. Gene lay flattened nearby. Heat waves from the blast beat down on his back, making him break out in a head-to-toe sweat.

A pillar of fire mushroomed into the sky. At its base was the white-hot wreckage of the truck, which skidded downward toward the knot of police cars. Doors flung open as the cars were abandoned *en masse* by their riders. But some doors were blocked or wouldn't open. A few of the quicker wits dove out the windows.

The truck had time enough to build up good momentum before slamming broadside into the clustered police cars. Spewed masses of flaming fuel and oil and sizzling metal showered the autos, igniting them into firebombs.

A string of explosions followed, drowning out the screams of those who were unable to escape, vaporizing them in an eyeblink. The avalanche of flaming metal tumbled down the hill with slow stateliness.

The lights of other police cars down below flashed into full brightness, their engines restarted. The few street lamps that were operable winked on. After a pause to comprehend the magnitude of the disaster, the surviving units once more began to stir, to advance.

Again, the lights dimmed as another blue globe took to the sky. The second lightning ball was smaller but more brilliant than the first. Faster, too. Streaking downhill, it zoomed toward the police cars stuck at the middle of the slope. The riders in the lead car got the hell out when they saw the blue ball coming. So did everybody else.

The target vehicle was engulfed in the heart of a blue-light sun. The sun turned red when the gas tank blew up, detonating a hell-bomb.

As soon as their cars started working again, what was left of the cops turned tail and retreated downhill.

Boyd pulled himself to his hands and knees at curbside. His ears rang and his bones ached but he had made it; he was alive. He had gotten out of the car just in time.

Monty hadn't.

Boyd shook his head to clear it, then saw Tracker standing about a dozen yards up the slope. Tracker and nobody else, not with those sunglasses at night. Boyd rubbed his eyes to make sure he wasn't seeing things. He wasn't, so he drew his gun. His hip was bruised from where he'd fallen against the weapon, but the neat little snub .38 Special was in perfect working order. Steadying it in a two-handed grip, he pointed it at Tracker's back. Tracker was busy helping a shaky little guy to his feet. The little guy looked familiar; Boyd had seen him around town.

He would die, too, as part of Boyd's anti-witness insurance plan.

As Boyd's finger tightened on the trigger, another blue light came into view. The size of a tennis ball, it was diamond-bright, radiant. It blazed at the tip of a portable launcher worn in a harness by a weird manlike figure who came striding down from the top of the hill. The weirdo had a bulbous helmeted head and thick gauntlets reaching to his elbows and padded boots with clunky thick soles.

Boyd hesitated, uncertain whether to kill Tracker first or the weirdo. Who was more dangerous?

Uncertainty was unknown to the operator in the insulation suit. Blueness outlined the weaponeer as the strange device was triggered.

A fist-sized blue lightning mini-ball sped toward Boyd. The apparatus had been improved in the weeks since the electrocution of absconding accountant Shepperd Judd.

Boyd yelped, snapped a shot at blue orb, missed.

It didn't.

The ball homed in on his gun, with its highly conductive metal parts. It burst on contact, discharging its prodigious store of agitated energy, fusing the gun into molten metal before the gunpowder in the bullets could explode. Unleashed torrents of raw electricity used the police lieutenant as the shortest route to ground, zapping him like a rat on a subway's live third rail.

Boyd fried.

The big flash lit up his skeleton like a blue X-ray before carbonizing it to an assemblage of brittle black sticks that crumbled into powder under the force of the blast. Boyd's after-image glowed bluely in midair for a few seconds more, further confounding the cops who'd survived the first fireball attack and flaming truck crash. They huddled nearby, awestruck by horror.

Boyd's remains looked like a heap of burnt toast scraps. Beneath them, the asphalt was melted and tarry, curling with thick noxious vapors.

A thunderclap cracked after the blast.

That did it. To a man, the cops jumped up and ran downhill.

The master of the lightning descended at a more leisurely pace, walking in the middle of the road with a ponderous stiffness suggestive of a deep-sea diver clomping about on the ocean floor.

The brown van glided to the hilltop's edge, covering him. Figures emerged from the darkness on both sides of the street, men mostly, but also a few women. Unlike their leader, they were more or less conventionally clad in cheap suits and dresses. All were armed, the majority with handguns and rifles, but a few with odd tube-shaped weapons that were held like guns.

Tracker had known the lurkers were there well before they showed themselves, thanks to his night vision and omnidirectional sonar. That's why he hadn't tried to use his gun on the lightning lord.

Gene stood on his knees near Tracker, unhurt but shaken, senses stunned, astonished.

Across the street, Mitch crouched on all fours in a vacant lot, motionless, staring. Not far from him was Vollin, who stood leaning against a tree for support. Blood ran down his face from a wound on his forehead.

A group of the newcomers trudged out of the woods behind the two gangsters and moved toward them, fanning out in a loose arc. They were stiff-limbed, intent, unspeaking, zomboid.

A similar group moved toward Tracker and Gene. Among them were the clownish redheaded woman and her sad sack mate who'd been handing out literature in front of the courthouse earlier that day. She was armed with one of the tubelike devices, he had a revolver. She was in charge of her group. The unique device fascinated Tracker, not least because its flaring bell-shaped mouth was pointed directly at him.

Vollin tensed, then elaborately relaxed, hands falling easily at his sides. "Don't, Vee," Mitch said in a voice so low he wasn't sure if Vollin had heard it.

A man held one of the tubelike devices leveled on Vollin and Mitch. Branton. A fist-sized bruise marked his jaw where Tracker had hit him before stealing his car.

Mitch edged away from Vollin.

The red-headed hag said, "Put down your weapons and you will not be hurt."

"Like hell!" Vollin said, and drew.

Both hands came up full with the twin .45s that had been stuffed in the top of his waistband. Maybe he thought the lightning lord wouldn't dare use his weapon for fear of hitting his followers, a shrewd guess but not the deciding factor.

Branton thumbed a switch on the tube, closing a circuit. A blue bolt leaped from the wide muzzle, spearing Vollin in the middle before he could shoot. Vollin was fast, but not lightning fast.

The blue bolt carried a mild charge compared to the mini-globe that had incinerated Boyd. The effect on Vollin was similar to having a live plugged-in TV set dropped into the tub while taking a bath: lethal.

Vollin froze statue-still, petrified, then toppled to the ground.

There was nothing in it for Tracker, they had him covered.

The muzzle of Branton's weapon glowed dull red, a redness that swiftly spread to the rest of the tube. Branton got rid of it fast, tossing it far away. It glowed bright red, liquefying into molten slag that burned deep into the soil.

So, the tubes were one time weapons, a fact mentally catalogued by Tracker for future reference.

Branton cursed, nursing some first-degree burns on his hand.

Tracker dropped the Uzi, Mitch put down his guns. Not having any guns, Gene held up his empty hands. Turning to face the energy weapon operator in the insulation suit, Tracker said, "Dr. Shock, I presume?"

"Not quite," the operator said, voice muffled by the helmet.

The helmet was unfastened and removed, unmasking its wearer: Anne Bellamy!

"The Master will see you now," she said.

16.

"ALL IS VANITY," the Master said. "Case in point: the considerable effort I've expended in keeping you alive long enough to attend this little meeting. Our last, I fear."

"Come again?" said Tracker.

"It was I who instructed my assistant, Miss Bellamy, to give warning of imminent attack."

"Sure, now I remember! The broad on the phone talked just like she does," Mitch said, pointing at Anne Bellamy. "It was her!"

"No more interruptions, my moronic mobster, or I'll vaporize you," the Master said. "To continue: my mobile electrosphere cannon saved you from the police when they surely would have had you. The portable projector in Miss Bellamy's capable hands discorporated the late unlamented Lt. Boyd, a vile creature who aroused in me a most profound loathing."

"If you wanted me alive, why did you shoot a lightning ball at me?"

"Lightning ball? Ah, yes, you must mean the electro-sphere. A most amusing phraseology, to be sure. I relied on your well-known athletic prowess to save you, and as always, I was right.

"And to what end was all this effort exerted? Why, simply that I might enjoy a few minutes brief communion with a kindred spirit capable of appreciating the greatness of my achievements. Although you have frittered away a genuine if modest talent on unscientific diversions, you are not entirely without understanding."

Tracker said, "You flatter me, Professor Moxon."

If there was sarcasm in Tracker's voice, Moxon chose to ignore it. He said, "Not at all. Some of your litte contraptions are quite clever in their way."

Moxon was Dr. Shock.

Owen Moxon, megalomaniac, crackpot idealogue, physicist of genius. Founder, master, and the most devout worshipper of a personality cult celebrating himself.

"Moxon? Isn't he the one who got kicked out of the Star Wars program for saying that people are like bugs?"

That's what the general public thought of Owen Moxon, if they bothered to think of him at all. The man the tabloids called "Dr. Shock." Some years back he'd been a ten-day media wonder thanks to a few candid comments he'd made near the close of a congressional subcommittee hearing on funding for the space-based Strategic Defense Initiative, "Star Wars" as it was popularly called.

Moxon was a titan in the field of Directed Energy Weapons, but his towering intellect did not suffer fools gladly, a fatal flaw when dealing with Congress. Near the end of a lengthy session testifying on the Hill, Moxon, intensely irritated by what he considered a waste of a day's worth of precious lab time, expressed the opinion that legislators unable to produce a balanced budget had no business ruling on complex scientific matters incomprehensible to their pea-brains. He also had a few choice words reserved for the voters who had sent such mental dimwits to Washington in the first place.

Actually, his most famous remark had been widely misquoted. "Public opinion is nothing more than the random buzzing of the national hive," was what he really said, but translated into tabloidese, the front page headlines screamed: DR. SHOCKER: "PEOPLE ARE BUGS."

The press and the public had fun with the "for-real mad scientist" bit for about ten days, then grew bored with it and dropped it like a hot potato. The media circus burned out, but Moxon was still too hot to handle. He'd given SDI's public image a black eye. Even those who secretly tended to agree with him wouldn't hire him, not even the top-secret R & D labs, for fear that word would somehow leak out and they'd be called before an investigating committee to explain his employment. Too many critics publicly quetioning his sanity led to the revocation of his security clearance, making him *persona non grata* at the Pentagon.

Moxon went away to the wilderness, not to meditate or mourn but to organize. City or country, the wilderness was always there, for it was the wilderness at the heart of lost souls hungry for something to believe in. He gave them Moxon to believe in. They gave him Higher Echelon, a fanatic cult dedicated to his doctrines, slavishly obedient to his every whim. His vehicle to power.

But people power was only a stepping stone to a higher power, the earthshaking power of chained lightning. Now he held that power firmly within his grasp. Plasma physics was his specialty, and the key to mastery of the secrets of Directed Energy. As recently as two decades ago, experts had debated the existence of ball lightning, despite centuries worth of folklore concerning the "fireballs," as they were popularly known. He, Moxon, had achieved the impossible, the creation of artificially generated ball lightning. That he used this epochal scientific discovery as an instrument of destruction was a telling comment on the gut-level human nature that Moxon professed to despise.

Tracker thought he knew the answer, but he asked the question anyway:

"Why all the killing?"

"Why? To smite the ungodly," Moxon said. "I hurl my avenging thunderbolts like Jove."

Some of his followers moaned then, overcome by religious rapture at hearing the Master pronounce his stern judgment.

"The unspeakable Yates and his creatures stole millions of dollars worth of Echelon revenues deposited in the Columbine and its affiliate banks. This criminal conspiracy not only stole my money with malice aforethought, it also betrayed every inhabitant of this planet by sabotaging the last best hope for the ultimate triumph of the human spirit against the forces of greed and stupidity."

"Which is?"

"Which is me," Moxon said. "Can you doubt it? As a scientist, you must realize the genius of my conception."

"I do," Tracker said. "The science is brilliant, but the application is a little crude."

"Crude is what people understand."

"Why your time and talent on a bloody vendetta against a gang of chiseling crooks? With an invention like that, you could write your own ticket."

"Don't be absurd. You know perfectly well that the destructive powers of the electro-sphere pale in comparison to its potential for delivering limitless amounts of clean efficient energy. The high-energy plasmoid sphere is the ideal matrix for controlled fusion reactions. Atomic hydrogen fusion—clean safe energy that could turn this madhouse planet into a paradise!

"What would happen if I offered my great invention as a gift to all mankind? It would cease to be my invention. The powers that be would take control of it to use and misuse it as they see fit. They'd sit on it and do nothing until the oil companies have wrung the last dollar out of the last drop of petroleum. Then they'd form committees and hold hearings and debate the pros and cons of atomic fusion in a democratic society while the world comes tumbling down all around them.

"Prometheus stole fire from the gods to warm the hearths of men. I bring down lightning from heaven to chill their souls! Reason and logic persuade the enlightened few. Fear motivates the masses. Very well, I shall teach them to fear the vengeance of my light that kills!

"In just a few more moments, a trembling world will witness the fateful lightning of my terrible swift sword," Moxon said.

Zero Hour was fast approaching.

Tracker took advantage of the break in Moxon's rantings to scan his surroundings in search of a loophole. The arena for the coming showdown was a flat-topped rocky promontory near a power trail on a ridge some two miles east of where Tracker had been captured.

The ridge ran east–west, with Redrow and the city to the north of it, and the edge of the plateau to the south. Both vistas could be seen from the promontory, which jutted out from the south side of the ridge. Where the plateau ended there was a deep valley with a highway winding through it, then more mountains.

The power trail crossed the ridge at right angles. A strip of land running north–south had been cleared up one side of the ridge and down the other. It was lined with a series of metal-framed power pylons strung with thick high-tension electric cables. The trail was posted with the electric company's NO TRESPASSING signs. There were no fences, no watchmen.

The hard stony ground on top of this part of the ridge was empty, untenanted. The nearest paved road was half a mile away. A dirt road connected it to the power trail.

The MEC—short for Mobile Electro-sphere Cannon, also known as the brown van—was parked on the promontory, facing southwest. Three other vehicles were parked nearby, two cars and a mini-van, all belonging to the Moxonites. After capturing Tracker, Mitch, and Gene, the cultists had loaded them in the cars and brought them here.

In addition to the prisoners, a baker's dozen of cultists occupied the site. Among them were Branton, Anne Bellamy, and Dotty and Russ Bainbridge (the clown-faced hag and her mate). They were in charge of the other, lesser Moxonites.

And there was Moxon.

Dr. Shock was taking no chances with Tracker. Tracker and the other two prisoners sat on the ground a stone's throw from the EMG battle wagon. Two guards armed with tubular shock-sticks kept watch on the prisoners. They stood flanking the van on both sides, commanding a clear field of fire in relation to the prisoners.

A speaker was mounted on the upper right rear corner of the MEC wagon. Tracker spoke to Moxon through it, Moxon spoke to Tracker through it. Moxon was inside the van compartment, speaking to Tracker through a transceiver on the instrument panel. The shielding that protected the vehicle from interference by its own hardware also rendered it impervious to all of Tracker's EMG probes.

Too bad. He'd have given his eyeteeth for a peek inside that treasure trove of advanced scientific wizardry.

The rank and file Moxonites bustled with activity, making ready for the big event. They never walked when they could run.

"Fucking whackos," Mitch muttered.

Gene said, "What—what do you think they'll do with us?"

"Nothing nice," Tracker said.

"It'll almost be worth it to get it over with and not have to listen to any more of that save-the-planet bullshit," Mitch said. He spoke out of side of his mouth, low-voiced, prison-wise, but the speaker must have had terrific audio pickup, since Moxon responded to his near-whispered comment.

"Saving the planet begins with the elimination of vicious antisocial hoodlums such as yourself," Moxon said. "However, I am not unmindful of the services you have unknowingly rendered me by your steadfast opposition to Yates."

"Does that mean I get out of this with a skin whole?"

"Be grateful that I prolong your miserable existence long enough to witness the annihilation of our mutual foe!"

"I'm thrilled."

"Focus your attention on the MEC's rooftop cannon. Observe the direction in which it is pointed. Draw an imaginary line from the muzzle across the valley to the other side. Where that line ends on the far mountain, look for an oval of light. Possibly you may be unable to see it due to adverse atmospheric considerations, but I assure you that it is there.

"Those are the lights of Ultima on Oldridge," Moxon went on, "Yates' stronghold. 'Ultima'—a grandiose name for what is little more than a bunker in a hole in the ground. Such hucksterism is characteristic of friend Yates."

Tracker knew the story of how the Oldridge site had been cleared and the labyrinthine foundations excavated right before the financing fell apart, cancelling the Ultima project. Yates stopped all construction except for a crash project to build a bunkerlike command post of poured concrete and reinforced steel in the most defensible section of the foundation. A grim hulking monolith from the outside, it was rumored to be a luxurious pleasure palace within. When Seven Cities' woes reached critical mass, Yates withdrew to the security of his bunker for the duration.

The site was guarded by a small private army. They controlled the single access road to Oldridge, which was protected by machine-gun nests, "smart" land mines, sensors, and other devices. The bunker was ringed with concentric trenches that could be filled with boiling oil, drawbridges, concertina wire, and antipersonnel devices by the score. Airborne attack by copter or plane was considered unlikely due to treacherous local air currents, but Ultima was prepared to meet that unlikely eventuality with sophisticated radar and heat-seeking surface-to-air missiles.

Ultima, a tough nut to crack. Apparently Moxon had given serious thought to the problem.

He continued, "Yates has let it be known among his contemptibles that he intends to stay inside the bunker until the crisis is passed. In the meantime, his cadre of paid assassins is busily eliminating anyone whom he perceives as a possible threat. Considering the universal unpopularity of the man, the murder purge should not be finished for some quite considerable length of time.

"The Unspeakable hides in his shell like a turtle and won't come out. Very well. Do you know how the eagle solves such a problem? The bird of prey takes hold of the turtle in its talons and flies to a great height before letting go. The turtles smashes on the rocks far below, cracking open its shell so the eagle can devour its tender flesh.

"I have devised a similar fate for the coyly retiring Mr. Yates. Like the eagle, I, too, will strike from above, but with a singular variation. Since I cannot bring Yates to the rocks of destruction, I will bring the rocks of destruction to him—an inhumation to be devoutly wished, to paraphrase the immortal Bard."

Mitch nudged Tracker, calling his attention to a group of the cultists hanging onto the words of Moxon with rapt devotion. They stood staring starry-eyed at the speaker broadcasting the Leader's chatty little talk.

"Look at the suckers soaking up that slop," Mitch said. "Chumps."

"Their master's voice."

Dotty Bainbridge shushed him. Her eyes glared and the veins stuck out on her neck.

Moxon said, "I regret that I cannot join with you all at this special time, but the complex nature of the pre-launch countdown demands that I remain at my post at the control board. I trust you will understand.

"For the benefit of our guests, I will review what is about to happen so they will better appreciate it. Presently, I will activate the Accumulator, the MEC's power source. In the simplest possible terms, the device is a receiver of wireless power, a sponge that soaks up electricity and stores it for later use. Generating no energy of its own, it steals the energy from all other power sources within its field. . . ."

The Accumulator was a machine with two basic components:

the Vampire, which produced the energy-eating field; and the Sponge, which stored the stolen power. The Vampire produced such side-effects as stopping cars dead, coronal and halo electrical phenomena, brownouts and blackouts, sparking, etc.

The Shaper was the core component of the apparatus, an incredibly tough and durable hollow cylinder, an EMG crucible where the raw stolen energy was processed into a coherent and self-sustaining whole, ready for use by the Delivery System.

The Delivery System included the launch mechanisms as well as the computerized range-finders and target-locators. The Template Chamber precipitated the high-energy plasmoid into three-dimensional space in the form of Nature's most perfect solid, the sphere. A certain degree of selectivity could be programmed into the orb by setting its internal vibratory cycle to a faster or slower pace. In electricity, opposites attract. Positive or negative, a charge seeks its mirror image. This truth was used to great effect in the lightning balls to give them a measure of "smartness," enabling them to distinguish between different targets. A plasmoid's vibratory rate impelled it to seek its complementary-charged counterpart. By adjusting the frequency up or down, the plasmoid could be set to attack the optimum target, be it man, beast or machine.

It was the first smart Directed Energy Weapon. It didn't belong to Washington or Moscow, capitalists or communists. It was the brainchild of a vengeful genius with an Overman complex and a sinister network of several thousand zomboid cultists in the U.S.A. and hundreds more abroad.

It would take more than lightning balls to crack the hardrock shell of W. Carson Yates.

"Extreme measures are required," Moxon said.

Tonight at midnight he would undertake the most dangerous gamble of his ill-starred career. A radical new technique for manipulating prodigious quantities of energy on a scale hitherto undreamed of would be set in motion to deliver the killing stroke to a hated foe. The process was risky, promising but still largely untried. Hazardous in the extreme. Victory or defeat, life or death hung in the balance.

At midnight.

17.

W. Carson Yates said, "I'm just a simple country boy from the Oklahoma oil patch—"

"Don't give me that, Carse," Sherry Hannock said. "There's no such thing as a *simple* country boy in the oil patch. The simple ones get weeded out fast."

"I know. That's why I'm here in Colorado," Yates cracked, slapping his thigh. "Told a good one on myself, didn't I?"

Mickey and Phil, his personal bodyguards, chuckled appreciatively. Many protectors were under hire to Yates, who needed protection. But Mickey and Phil held a special status. As his personal bodyguards, they went everywhere he did. Everywhere. When he had to go to the bathroom, one of them first gave the bathrom the once-over for booby traps and electronic bugging devices, then the other waited outside the door until Yates was done.

Mickey and Phil were two peas out of the same pod. They were built like pro footballers and watchful as Secret Service agents. Mickey was blond and Phil was dark-haired; that was the only difference between them.

Yates was big and doughy. What hair he had left was cut and styled by a hair stylist brought in from Aspen once a week. His nails were manicured, he had a sun lamp tan. He was flabby. The only exercise he was getting up here at Ultima was eating gourmet meals. He was getting plenty of that. Some days he ate four or five meals. He was getting fat. His big gut strained the buttons of his custom-tailored rhinestone cowboy shirt. Belly rolls slopped over the top of his hand-tooled leather belt. His chunky oversized belt buckle cut into his blubber so deeply that sometimes the upper half of it was lost from sight.

"I'm just a simple country boy who built the world's fanciest gilded cage and locked myself up in it," Yates said. "And I'm not coming out, either. I've got everything I need right here. Good food, good booze, good company, a good-looking woman—"

"Good cover," said Chet Rollo.

"Yeah, that too. Last but not least. No loco cowboys and mob greaseballs trying to shoot my ass," Yates said.

Sherry leaned forward, reaching for her drink on the marble inlaid coffee table. It was something sweet and pink and frothy in a long tall glass. She was a gorgeous redhead, broad-shouldered, big-breasted, long-legged, sheathed in a short tight emerald silk dress. "Some birdcage," she said, looking around the vast creamy expanses of the sunken living room. "This place makes the lobby of the Plaza hotel look like a broom closet."

"By now it just may be a broom closet, what with all the hard times they've been having lately in New York City," Chet Rollo said. He was Yates' chief administration henchman in charge of skullduggery and conspiracy. Not his official title, but an accurate description of his job duties. He was fine-featured, forty, and fit, but too much sun had weathered his face until it looked ten years older than it actually was.

"I don't care if Manhattan is falling apart, I'd like to go there anyway," Sherry said. "I'd like to go someplace, anyplace at all."

"Stop whining," Yates said, suddenly hard-faced, serious.

Some of the color drained from Sherry's face. "Sorry, Carse, really. That just slipped out; I don't mean anything by it."

"Shut up."

Safely unseen behind the boss' back, Mickey and Phil exchanged knowing glances.

"You don't have to go across the country to see a town go into the toilet," Chet said. "Just watch Mountain City tear itself apart."

Yates said, "I love to watch those idiots whomping on each other, knocking their brains out to keep their miserable little pieces of turf. I'm up here, safe and sound, sitting it out while the gangs wipe each other out. When the dust finally settles, there won't be anything of them left but a rag and a bone and a hank of hair."

"Good riddance," Chet said.

"Then I'll be king of the hill."

"You're already that, Carse," Sherry said.

"Quit trying to butter me up."

"You are *so* mean! Anyway, it's true. You are so the king of the hill, you said so yourself the other day."

Yates decided to laugh instead of get madder. "Okay, then I'll be king of the valley, too," he said. "And the king of Mountain City."

"No problem," Chet said. "You've got all the money in town already."

They had no hesitancy in discussing sensitive matters in front of the bodyguards. Confidentiality and absolute discretion as regards the client is standard operating procedure for protectors at Mickey and Phil's high level of the profession.

Yates said, "Those oldtime dukes and lords and such had the right idea with their castles. Make your home a fortress and make your fortress a home and you can't go wrong."

"I'll embroider that on a sampler and hang it up on the wall," Sherry said.

"Ease up on the sauce, you're getting sloppy."

"Sorry, Carse."

The phone rang. Actually it didn't ring, it made electronic burblings and bleepings to announce an incoming call. An attractively designed portable cordless phone, it sat on the coffee table.

"What time have you got, Chet?"

"About five to midnight."

"Right on time. The big professor must want to cut a deal pretty bad."

"I'm not so sure, Carse," Chet said. "That old boy is one very spooky old dude. He's cracked. And those followers of his—ugh!"

Yates picked up the phone, his free hand flicking the air as if to brush aside Chet's misgivings.

"Howdy, Prof. How's tricks?"

"Oh, I've got one or two that may surprise you, Yates."

"You've got to get up pretty early in the morning to do that. I don't keep banker's hours, you know."

"Ha ha. No, just their assets."

"We're not going to get anywhere going over the same old ground. I thought you were willing to talk sense for a change. Keeping in mind that I won't say anything over the phone that I wouldn't be willing to testify to in court."

"You seem to be an expert on the subject."

"I try, Prof. Of course, I don't have your kind of expertise with big league congressional investigating committees, but I get by. Say, that was a terrible business down to the courthouse this morning, terrible business. Awful."

"Yes, how unfortunate that Sullivan was killed before he could testify. I was looking forward to his performance on the witness stand."

"Looks like he's going to be a no-show."

"He'll be missed. As will the late liquidated Lt. Boyd. He was struck by lightning, they say. Strange . . . a number of your associates have died in just that way—killed by lightning, I mean. When you consider the odds against being hit by lightning, the chances of its happening a half-dozen times in six weeks, and all to members of your intimate circle, well, it's food for thought."

"You didn't call me up to talk about the weather, Prof. Let's get down to business or call it a night. You're already up way past your bedtime."

"History is made at night, so they say. And I certainly wouldn't be so rude as to miss the chance of wishing you a heartfelt *adieu*. You're about to become a part of history, Yates."

"Wait a minute, Prof, are you threatening me? Because that's a crime, and the police would have to get involved, and I'd hate to send a cracked but harmless old coot like you to the pokey."

"The police are understaffed right now. A number of vacancies have suddenly opened up in the department."

"I'll send flowers."

"Save them for yourself."

"I'll put them on your grave, Prof, after I get done pissing on it. That'll be soon, I think—you being an old man and all."

"You're in your grave now, Yates. Like the pharoahs of old,

you'll be entombed amidst all your worldly goods. A fitting fate for the pharaoh of the money pyramid.

"I must go now. The phones will be useless when the machines are switched on a minute from now. When your world comes crashing down, remember that the demolisher was I, Owen Moxon—your master!"

Moxon broke the connection before Yates could reply.

Yates frowned at the receiver in his hand. "Weird!" he said.

Chet said, "Something wrong?"

"The prof's loonier than a drunken bat. All that radiation he worked with must have soaked in his brain, softened it up," Yates said.

The phone screamed.

An ear-splitting feedback shriek yowled out of both ends of the receiver. It wouldn't stop. It worked on the nerves like a dentist's drill. Yates threw it against the wall, shattering the plastic shrouding. The yowling continued. Sherry put her hands over her ears. Other electrical equipment started malfunctioning, taking on a life of its own. The 72-inch wall-mounted giant TV screen turned itself on and off, strobing like a twitching eyelid. Stereos, CD players blatted discordant blasts of sound. The lights flickered. Still covering her ears, Sherry wailed, "Oh God, what's happening?!"

Two minutes to midnight.

Titanic energies began to stir on top of the ridge. A low ceiling of dark clouds covered the sky. Trees shook their branches and tossed their boughs, though no breezes blew.

The energization process had begun.

The fires in Redrow's old industrial section had been extinguished, except for a few stubborn hot spots, but new blazes leaped up in five or six places north of Rowe Street. Riots had broken out on the Strip, looting, arson. The anarchy raged unchecked because different factions of the police department made war on each other in the streets.

The stony ridge top was dark, desolate, isolated from the chaos down below. But already it was breeding its own brand of chaos, born of machine wizardry and raw power surging through the lines.

There was a portable phone in the MEC wagon. Moxon had completed his call to Yates within a minute or two before midnight. He then had a last word with the prisoners, who sat on a log facing the promontory.

They were in the center of a clearing with lots of space surrounding them and no cover to hide in. They were not under restraint, but their guards were careful to stay well outside the range of one of Tracker's kinetic flying kicks. His martial arts abilities were known and effectively countered by their security arrangements.

Moxon, too, was careful to keep his distance from Tracker. He was flanked with a pair of vigilant protectors, one male, the other female, both equally stone-faced as they eyed the captives for the sign of a reason to blast them.

Moxon said, "You can guess why I've spared your life up to now, Major Tracker. There is a chance that this experiment may fail, although my calculations say otherwise. Even Jove nods. Failure could become disaster, catastrophe. If I should die, there will be a measure of comfort in knowing that a trained scientific observer will have witnessed the proceedings and can credibly report the truth."

"And if you succeed?"

"Then I shall have a lever with which to move the world," Moxon said. "Your position would be rather awkward, though."

"In that case, you'll undersand why I don't wish you luck."

"Quite. No matter what the result, one of us must surely die."

"All men must die."

"An appropriate slogan for this enterprise. Farewell, Major. I think it unlikely that we shall meet again."

"So long," Tracker said.

Moxon turned on his heels and strode toward the MEC wagon, the overcoat draped across his shoulders flapping like a cape.

The MEC wagon was already cycling, building up the power to generate the Vampire's energy-absorbing fields. A watery blue aura outlined the vehicle. A Moxonite stood at the ready to open the van's rear hatch at the Leader's approach. The cultist performed the task with ceremonial stiffness, formality. The hatchway slid partly open, opening the lid on a mass of glittering instruments and machinery. Consoles lined both walls. There was a curved control panel with display screens, dials, gauges. The operator's chair faced it, secured to the floor. A cylindrical shaft suggestive of a submarine's periscope mounting stretched from the rubber-carpeted floor to the bubble dome in the roof.

The overriding impression was a tantalizing combination of familiar, obscure, and unknown technology synthesized into new and exciting arrangements. Moxon's long exile from mainstream Big Science had caused him to develop uniquely personalized hardware. There was too much happening for the mind to comprehend at a glance, even a trained mind like Tracker's. He didn't have to, not when his video eyes devoured the scene and input it to the computer's circuitry, storing it in memory.

Solemn servitors helped Moxon prepare for the event. He donned an insulation suit, padded boots, helmet, thin rubber gloves. The protective garment was considerably more lightweight than the one worn by the portable launcher operator.

With a final salute, Moxon stepped up into the MEC wagon and fitted himself into the curved, padded operator's chair. He fastened his shoulder and lap restraint belts. Gloved hands curled poised over the keyboard, then began throwing switches, pressing buttons, setting dials. White-green sine waves seesawed across dull green oscilloscope screens. The hatchway slid down to seal the vehicle. Servomotors whirred, metal brackets dogged shut.

Strange things started happening.

The Vampire's field generator boosted its output, expanding the invisible lines of force. This start-up process consumed the most energy of any sequence in the complete launch cycle. It drew its power from the reserves stored in the Sponge component of the Accumulator. They were drained nearly dry before the Vampire field reached the critical threshold where it began to take in more power than it lost. At that point it became self-sustaining.

Never before had the Vampire tapped into a power source as dynamic as the river of electricity flowing through the cables of the power trail, a Niagara of energy. The kind of power needed to crack Yates' shell.

Outside, winds began to blow, gusting from different directions. Gene said, "What kind of storm is it when the wind blows north, then south?"

"A shitstorm," Mitch replied.

The pylon towers nearest to the top of the ridge began to take on a hard metallic glitter, deep blue. Blue coronas ringed the tops of the towers, and their skeletal frameworks seemed rimmed with blue hoarfrost. Sparks snapped in the air, on the crossbars of the towers, skittering across the tops of the cables. Energy from the power lines strained to break free and merge with the oppositely charged Vampire field. The leading edges of the two fields pulsated, quivered, touched. Cataracts of electricity poured into the cyclonic force funnel. The lights of Mountain City and its environs flickered, wavered, dimmed.

"It's midnight," Tracker said.

The MEC wagon shuddered with vibrations, buzzing and humming. A ghostly whirling blue cloud engulfed it.

The scene on the ridge was wild. Winds boomed, trees flailed, pylons reeled, and electricity crackled in the air.

The basic MEC model could not long have endured this kind of overload, but Moxon had customized this wagon to meet the challenge. The challenge of tapping into a river of raw energy and diverting it to destroy a seemingly impregnable fortress.

No Accumulator or battery of Accumulators could dam that flow of energy, not for a nano-second. They'd be obliterated, vaporized along with the rest of the MEC wagon. But this MEC wagon had been rebuilt to channel that tremendous energy. Instead of being poured into Sponge reservoirs, the stolen power would be discharged as fast as it was absorbed. To this end, the MEC was fitted with a stronger, simpler beam projector. It wasn't fancy but it could take a lot of punishment. The projector nozzle was trained on Ultima on a mountain across the valley. The usual computerized coordinate system kept the weapon on target.

The vehicle rocked from the impact of all that power surging through it. The beam cannon came to life, roaring at full blast. Blue-white lightning and noise burst from the muzzle, spearing across the valley and into Ultima on Oldridge. Where it emerged from the nozzle, the beam was as wide as a man's body. Internal stabilizers fought a constant battle against the beam's tendency to scatter in the air. White lightnings as big as rattlesnakes curled around the blue beam. Quantitites of exhilirating ozone invigorated the air.

What Moxon had done was like tapping Niagara Falls to put out a house afire. The blue beam jetted out of the projector like water from a hose. Moxon sprayed Ultima with it. Blue lightning licked the site, playing over it. Rocks shattered, trees carbonized, half-built walls and shells of half-built buildings were bowled over and leveled.

Not enough. The bunker was hunkered down in one of the excavated foundations, below the line of fire of the lightning beam. It would probably survive intact and relatively unharmed, spared as it was from the menace of direct hits.

Moxon took pleasure in imagining the nightmare scenario now being enacted inside the bunker as its electrical systems went berserk under the onslaught of annihilating energy.

Not enough. After sweeping the construction site with the beam, Moxon uptilted the projector's muzzle. The blue beam obeyed the cannon's prompting, tearing upward into the cliffs behind and above Oldridge. He locked in on a boulder as big as a house a hundred feet above Oldridge. Using the beam head, he carved the boulder out of the rocks with lightning. The boulder crashed down on Ultima, bringing plenty more rocks with it, each of them as big as houses. They bombarded Oldridge.

Using the beam as a rockcutter, Moxon played it over a section of jutting cliff buttress. Blasting stones, cracking rocks, carving off long vertical slabs of rock. The avalanche skidded down the cliffside, stopping to bury Oldridge under a few hundred feet of rocks and soil, and Ultima along with it.

"I hurl my avenging thunderbolts like Jove!"

18.

But even Jove nods.

Moxon made one small error, a mistake in judgment. He let the lightning beam run a few seconds too long. That was all, but it was enough. Had he shut down the beam right after using it to bury W. Carson Yates and company under a few hundred tons of earth and stone, all would have been well.

But he didn't. He paused to admire the scenes of rockfalls and landslides and Ultima's premature burial pictured on the control console's video display monitors. The beam continued to operate at full blast, spewing torrents of raw force at the same spot on the far cliffs. Stone splintered, cracked, shattered, softened, melted. Molten rock cascaded down the mountain. The rocks under the beam head vitrified, becoming as smooth as glass. It had a certain reflective quality that destabilized the beam head by bouncing some of its energy athwart the light path. The beam had a tendency to scatter, and this finished the job.

The beam split in two.

It all came apart in a very few seconds. But seconds are eons when time is measured in nano-seconds, the clock speed of computer processes. In the few heartbeats' worth of time that it took Moxon to perceive the danger, the damage had already been done.

The split beams scissored, cutting across each other.

Backlash!

The disruption sent a shock wave backblasting up the line, rippling up the beam to the projector. The muzzle split in quarters, bending back like a banana peel.

The beam went rogue wild, out of control. It split into a dozen smaller mini-bolts, crackling and flailing like bullwhips of blue electric light. Tentacles tangled, wove nets of light, ripped apart. The bolts scourged the promontory and the top of the ridge. At their touch trees burst into flame, rocks were pulverized.

"Here's our chance to make a break!" That's what Mitch intended to say to Tracker, but when he turned his head to speak, Tracker was gone.

A few yards to the side, there was a desperate struggle between Tracker and Branton. The spectacular disaster had furnished Tracker with all the diversion he needed.

Rays of all shapes and sizes shafted from the peeled-back projector barrel of the MEC wagon. Sizzling beams shot into the sky, sliced the tops off trees, slanted into the ground and bounced off rocks.

Branton had one of the tubular shock sticks. He was swinging it across his body to get it into play but Tracker got there first. They collided front to front. Branton was solid clear through. Tracker was inside the other's right arm, fighting for the weapon.

Most of the Moxonites had all they could do just to stay alive in that madhouse bedlam of crackling blue lightning, strobing lights, fire, noise, and chaos. But two of those who'd been guarding the prisoners rushed Tracker and Branton. They had guns but didn't want to use them for fear of hitting Branton.

Tracker clutched the wrist of Branton's weapon hand, turning it so the weapon was leveled at the two guards who were rushing him. He got his finger on the control stud and thumbed it on. "No!" one of the guards shrieked before he and his partner were scythed by a fan-shaped jet of dirty blue-yellow energy vented by the shock stick. They burst into human torches, straw men tossed on a bonfire.

Tracker clamped a hand over Branton's, crushing it against the shock stick so he couldn't let go. The weapon was already heating up; its bell mouth blazed a bright cherry red.

The shock stick was a one-shot deal, a high-voltage equivalent to a derringer; use once and throw away. Quickly, because the crude storage cell that allowed it to carry one charge autodestructed immediately after use. Moxon was jealous of his secrets falling into other hands; therefore he ensured that those hands would be burned off at the wrists if said owners reached too greedily for depleted shock sticks.

Tracker and Branton wrestled standing up. Branton was big, solidly planted, not easily dislodged. Fierce heat radiated from the red glowing weapon. Branton tried to shake Tracker loose, but Tracker held on with a bulldog grip. Tracker was starting to feel the heat, and he held Branton's hand between his own flesh and the shock stick, red now from stem to stern.

Branton crowded Tracker too close, trying to yoke his left arm around Tracker's throat. Tracker snapped his head backward, popping Branton square in the face with a reverse head butt. Branton was a hard man; he took the hit with a grunt and kept fighting. There was a sizzling sound, the hiss of Branton's hand scorching against the hot metal.

Tracker backed Branton into a tree, slamming him. He did it again. There was the smell of burning flesh.

Branton shrieked. He went wild, clawing at Tracker's face with his left hand. His fingertips hooked into the left earpiece and came close to tearing loose the opti-visor. It would have come off already if it wasn't secured by small needlelike jacks plugged into pinhead-sized sockets surgically implanted in the bones of his eye sockets. They stayed on, barely, but Tracker didn't like anybody messing with his glasses. He twisted Branton's right arm at an acute angle, reversing suddenly, twisted the forearm, and shoved the hand with the shock tube into his face as the meltdown began.

Tracker jumped back to avoid flying gobbets of molten metal. A few droplets splashed on the bottom of one of his pant legs, burning through the fabric in an eyeblink, but missing his flesh.

Branton shrieked his agony. His face was shrouded in a mass of melted metal and flesh. A hardball-sized lump of angry red metal, part of the shock stick, was fused to the scorched stump of his gun hand. Stumbling and screaming, Branton lurched out from behind the trees into the clearing. A shot was fired. Branton fell down dead.

"Call me a softie, but I hate to see a guy suffer," Mitch said, stepping into view with a gun in his hand. "I picked this up off of one of the stiffs," he said. "Wish I had me a dozen more—*hey*!"

Tracker dove, tackling Mitch, knocking him flat to the ground. Bullets ripped overhead at wasit-height, riddling trees and bushes. Wood chips sprayed, leafy branches fell.

The shooter was Russ Bainbridge. He stood half-hidden by a small stand of trees on the far side of the clearing, diagonally across from Tracker and Mitch. Russ had a hunting rifle with a long clip and was firing semiauto. He fired a few more shots but the tree trunks interfered with the rifle barrel, denying him a clear line of fire.

Mitch raised himself on his elbows, off his back. He threw some lead at Russ, narrowly missing him. One bullet was so close that it drilled a corner of his loose flapping shirt, lifting it.

Russ yelped, ducking behind the trees. He stumbled over a root, lost his balance, dropped the rifle, and fell.

Mitch couldn't see him but he put another slug into the middle of the trees anyway for good measure. Didn't sound like it hit anything but wood. He fired two more shots in that direction to cover Tracker and himself as they retreated from the open spaces to the thick tangled scrub brush that edged the clearing. They dove headfirst into the thicket and crawled a dozen yards deeper before stopping. Tracker said, "Where's Gene?"

"One of them lightnings hit pretty near us and knocked me on my ass. When I got up again and looked around, he was gone," Mitch said. "He's probably hightailed it halfway to Mountain City by now."

"Maybe."

"The fireworks back in Redrow were something, but this show has 'em beat by a country mile," Mitch said, relishing the pyrotechnics with childlike glee.

The MEC wagon squatted on the promontory like an octopus clinging to a rock, an octopus with a mechanical body and tentacles of blue lightning. Curling neon blue tendrils, whipsawing, flailing, beating the rocky ground. Whenever they touched stone they tore into it like jackhammers, cracking it, whipping up clouds of dust and stone chips. The wagon was a battered hulk poised on its wheelbases since the tires had all burst. The van box was dented and sprung open at the edges. The rear hatchway was jammed shut except for a narrow space at the bottom about twelve inches wide.

The Accumulator was jammed, too, jammed open so that the Vampire field continued to guzzle energy from the power lines, fueling the MEC wagon's continuing self-destruction. The beamer was still on but the projector was a useless wreck, venting wild shapes and streamers of neon-blue light. Dragons, snakes, spirals, banners, birds, and butterflies were only a few of the shapes suggested by the blazing blue inferno.

Rushing winds scoured the ridge, black clouds boiled above it. Bright blue pylons along the power trail swayed and snaked like a conga line, enveloped in a milky blue-white haze.

Five surviving Moxonites stood as close as they dared to the MEC wagon, lining up side by side at the place where the rocky knob jutted outward from the edge of the ridge. They stood facing the wagon, their backs to the ridge. Dottie and Russ Bainbridge were there, and three others. Anne Bellamy was not among them. Where was she?

More important, what had become of the portable beam launcher, the mid-sized DEW model she had wielded to such devastating effect?

And Moxon, what of him? Surely nothing human could have survived for more than an instant in that raging maelstrom of runaway energy that engulfed the MEC vehicle. But Moxon's scientific genius transcended ordinary human norms. The master of the lightning might even have discovered the secret of staying alive at the heart of the vortex.

Tracker's EMG probes were unable to reach beyond the surface of the superbly shielded MEC wagon to delve into its hidden mysteries.

The power line pylons were hung with strings of beaded glass insulators. Each bead was as big as a basketball. Now, they began to melt like wax. Blazing blue pylons wavered, reeling. Live cables tore free from their mountings, spitting blue sparks as they whipsawed. More cables tore loose, flogging the ground with electric fire. It seemed to take forever for the first pylon to fall, but once it did the others fell in line like dominoes.

Mountain City plateau blacked out. The roaring winds immediately lessened.

Denied its power source, the blue vortex engulfing the MEC wagon should have diminished, faded, and died. That was Tracker's logical assumption, and it was wrong. The reverse occurred. The vortex grew bigger and stronger and more brilliant. Spinning like a top, it set the winds whirling.

The last five cultists joined hands and started walking across the promontory toward the MEC.

"Are they nuts?" Mitch said, goggling.

The cyclonic blue vortex rose from the MEC like a genie released from a magic lantern. It was a twister, an EMG tornado. Funnel-shaped. Parts of it rotated at different speeds, giving it a perilous, herky-jerky slant, as if it was in danger of coming apart at the slightest touch. Blue bolts spat from it as it spun, exploding where they struck the rocks. A maypole with lightning bolts for streamers.

The five cultists advanced steadily at a deliberate pace, flinching as the bolts struck nearer to them, but not stopping or even slowing much. One of them panicked at the halfway mark, broke, and ran back toward the ridge. Russ Bainbridge. He didn't get far before being cut down, not by lightning, but by an old-fashioned bullet in the back.

His wife was his executioner. She waited to see whether or not he'd need another bullet. He didn't. She placed her gun on the rocks at her feet, joined hands with the others, and resumed the procession.

Cracks opened where the promontory jutted out from the ridge, separating them with a crevice four feet wide and forty feet deep. The cultists hesitated, halted, still holding hands. Some looked back. More cracks appeared, splintering the rocks, netting the knob with a spidery black web.

Battered by a barrage of hyper-energetic bolts as big as ten-ton snakes, the rocky knob broke off from the ridge and fell away.

With it went Moxon, the MEC wagon, the vortex, and the cultists.

19.

THE LAST ECHOES of the crash were still fading when Tracker and Mitch went to the cliff edge to inspect the damage. Where the promontory had been was now only emptiness, fifteen hundred feet of it straight down. Tracker said, "Careful of the edge, Mitch. Some of this new ground's not so solid."

"Hell, I'm half mountain goat—*whoa*!" A piece of ground gave way under Mitch's foot. He lurched forward. Tracker grabbed him under the arms and pulled him back hard. They took a few steps backward, somehow their feet got tangled, and Mitch found himself sitting on solid ground. "What'd I tell you, Major? Half mountain goat!"

"Which half?"

Tracker lay down on solid rock and bellied to the edge and looked down. Far below lay rugged mountain country, thickly wooded, uninhabited. Not a speck of electric blue light showed itself in the night landscape. A ghostly cloud of dust kicked up by the crash drifted lazily upward.

Tracker's beams went plunging downward, lancing through darkness and murk. He detected no unusual radiation, no traces of the MEC wagon, no survivors. The knob had turned once or twice during the fall, so it was quite possible that Moxon, his machines, and his minions were buried under tons of fallen rock. Too deep for him to detect via his IR and other EMG scans. Tracker turned and lowcrawled back to solid ground before standing up. He straightened out his clothes, brushed dirt off his knees. "Exit Moxon," he said.

Mitch said, "Some finish! But what do we do for an encore?"

"Die."

They turned at the sound of the voice behind them, Mitch swiftly and Tracker with more deliberateness. Gene stood twenty feet away, pointing a shotgun at them.

"Whew!" Mitch said. "You gave me a start, squirt. For a second there, I thought there was one of 'em that we'd missed."

"There is."

"Yeah, who?"

"Killer Gordon," Gene said.

Mitch chewed that over. "Say, you've got a gun. I never saw you with no gun before, squirt."

"It's not my style, but sometimes you've got to be flexible."

Tracker said, "What *is* your style, Gene?"

"Haven't you guessed it yet, Shades?"

"I think so."

"Then you know that you've got to die, both of you. *Now*."

Mitch said, "What is this, a gag?"

"No gag, Mitch," Tracker said. "Don't you get it yet? *He's Killer Gordon.*"

"The squirt? Nuts!"

"Well now, Mitch, you can call me squirt, or you can call me Gene, or you can call me Gordon, or you can call me Gene Gordon, or you can call me Killer."

"Naw, can't be, not in a million years. You, the guy who's been sharpening pencils and emptying wastebaskets for years down at the union hall while everybody else moved up to the big scores?"

"Can you think of a better front? Nobody cares about a small-time chiseler, not the cops or the crooks. I blend into the background. Some of the sweetest hits I've ever made have come from choice bits of news from loudmouths like you, Mitch. Guys who are too dumb to keep their traps shut in front of guys like me."

Tracker said, "You had me fooled."

"Don't take it too badly, Shades. That's what happens when you go up against a professional. I planned the courthouse murders, I put together the string to do the hit, and I had the place staked out to keep an eye on things when you showed up. I even rigged it so Mitch thought I was stooging for him. I decided to keep an eye on you. I'd have run away first if I'd known what kind of a job this would turn out to be."

"Why kill us now? Your boss is dead. It's over."

"Professionalism. Trade ethics and all that. Yates paid me in full in advance to hit you and Mitch. A contract is a contract, even if the client dies. So now you die," Gene said.

Tracker said, "You forgot two things."

"No stalls, Shades. I've heard them all. It's unworthy of you. Besides, why postpone the inevitable? I'll make it quick and painless, I promise you that."

Mitch said, "You a dentist or a hitman?"

"I've filled plenty of holes, the kind they put dead people in. I've reserved two on the aisle for you at the local graveyard."

Tracker said, "The first thing you forgot is Anne, Moxon's lady hatchet man. She's still alive."

Gene groaned, making a sour face.

"You're not going to pull that old routine, are you Shades? Not the oldest gag in the book, the one where even though I know there's nobody behind me I'm dumb enough to look anyway so you can rush me. I better finish this off now before you make with the sob stories about your wife and seven kids and gray-haired old mother."

A diamond-bright blue light shone somewhere in the middle distance behind Gene.

"Well, I'll be," Mitch said.

The light was bright enough for Gene to see its blueness glowing all around him, on Mitch and Tracker. Gene, worried, wanted to look over his shoulder at the blue light source, but was afraid to take his eyes off Tracker and Mitch. "This won't change anything," he said nervously.

"Not for us. She's got every reason for wanting Mitch and me dead. Sure screws up your plans, though."

Mitch said, "Let's see you get yourself out of this one, squirt."

Gene's grip tightened on the stock and pump of the riot shotgun.

"Save those shells for the lightning ball," Tracker said. "I've got a theory that if you put enough lead into it, it won't be able to stabilize its shape and will blow up. That's only a theory, of course, but it's worth a try."

"Deal," Gene said. "You're smart, Shades. Figure something out. Talk to her, maybe she'll listen to you."

"Be ready when that fireball comes swooping in. Don't miss. There won't be a second chance."

"Shit!"

"We make a perfect target all together like this," Tracker said. "If we spread out, that's three targets. Two might make it out alive. There's jumping off the cliff, if you don't feel like burning."

"You crazy—"

"The fireball! Shoot, SHOOT!"

Tracker's panicked shout galvanized Gene, who swiveled around, swung the shotgun up, pointed it toward the sky—

Tracker reached behind his back and drew the flat black automatic pistol he'd hidden in his waistband at the small of his back.

Gene found no fireballs in the immediate vicinity. He knew he'd been had.

Tracker shot him three times in the head. Once would have been enough, but Tracker wasn't taking any chances.

"Don't fight a war on two fronts. That is the second thing you forgot," Tracker said. "But that's what happens when you go up against a professional."

Mitch pried the weapon from Killer Gene Gordon's hands.

"Shoot if you have to, but don't start anything first," Tracker said. "Let's see if she's friend or foe."

The blue light was the focusing orb in the bore of the portable beam launcher now being wielded by Anne Bellamy. She stood in front of two cars and a mini-van parked under some trees on the far side of the clearing. She pointed the beam launcher at them, they pointed their guns at her. Nobody moved. Each waited for the other side to make an aggressive move that would trigger the showdown. A tense stalemate resulted. Deadlock.

A moment more, and then she withdrew, covering them as she left the scene, disappearing behind the cars. The mini-van started up, dark but for its parking and brake lights. It shouldered onto the gravel road leading west, driving at about ten miles per hour.

"Whew! That was a lucky break. Why didn't she blast us when she had the chance?"

"Remember Moxon's last instructions, Mitch. If the experiment was a failure and he was killed, he wanted independent witnesses to tell his story to the world."

"Why?"

Tracker shrugged. "Ego, maybe. Show the world he was as smart as he thought he was. Or maybe it was his scientific zeal to get the facts on the record for the benefit of future generations of researchers to follow in his footsteps. I'd like to think it was the latter, but who knows?"

The mini-van halted when it was a hundred yards away on the gravel road.

"Uh-oh, maybe we spoke too soon," Mitch said.

The portable launcher lofted a lightning mini-ball into the grove where the cars were parked. A second followed on its heels, leaving both autos wrecked and burning.

"Smart. Now we can't follow her."

"I wasn't too keen on that anyway, Major."

The mini-van vanished into darkness.

Mitch said, "How about Killer Gordon turning out to be the squirt, for crying out loud? The little punk! You sure didn't leave him much of a head. Nice shooting."

"My pleasure."

"But where'd you get the gun? Back when we was hiding in the trees, you said you didn't have one. You wouldn't be taking out some insurance against old Mitch, now would you, Major?"

"It's yours," Tracker said, handing Mitch the weapon butt-first.

"Huh? You're right, that's my gun, but where did you get it? I didn't even know I'd lost it until the squirt braced us and I felt around for it and it wasn't there."

"I took the liberty of lifting it from you when I was giving you a hand back at the cliff."

"Why, you dirty—"

"Ah-ah, Mitch. Remember that you're talking to an officer and a gentleman."

"Gentleman? You're a thief!"

"Only in a good cause. I thought I saw someone sneaking around, following us, but I wasn't sure. I didn't want to tip my hand and risk scaring him off, so I played dumb and sneaked your gun so he wouldn't know I had it."

Tracker's explanation was accurate as far as it went, but it omitted certain key facts. His videosonics made it difficult if not impossible for him to be taken by surprise or stealth. Omnidirectional sonar had warned him of someone sneaking around behind his back. Night vision plus magnification optics allowed him to pinpoint the location not only of Gene but of Anne

Bellamy, too. When he'd finally dealt himself into the big game, the deck was already stacked in his favor, with the winning hand in his pocket and a few hole cards up his sleeve.

But why confuse Mitch with the facts? Besides, national security regulations prohibited him from revealing classified information to unauthorized personnel. He made sure to empty Mitch's gun before giving it back to him. Mitch wasn't a bad sort for a murderous racketeer and gang chieftain, but there was no sense in leading him to temptation.

"You're the first guy who ever skunked me and made me like it, Major," Mitch said, "but don't try it again."

"Not to worry. My job here is done, and I'll soon be long gone."

"You ain't going nowhere without a car, unless you figure on walking back to town. Me, I've had enough exercise for one night."

"We can hitch a ride from the power company linemen when they show up here to investigate the blackout."

"What about the cops?"

"After tonight, there won't be enough officers left in the Mountain City Police Department to make a decent donut run."

"Yeah," Mitch said. "Yeah, a town without cops won't be too hard to take. That's my kind of town!"

Tracker didn't have the heart to tell Mitch what he already knew, thanks to monitoring the radio traffic through his wideband scanner:

Mountain City was now under martial law. Earlier tonight, after an eleventh-hour meeting with a hastily convened advisory board of respected law enforcers (including Bullet Bob Martinez), the Governor had decreed a state of emergency and called out the National Guard to restore law and order.

Moonlight shone through a hole in the clouds, silvering the mountain peaks.

"Look," Mitch said, pointing across the valley. "See that ledge, about two-thirds of the way up that mountain? That's Oldridge, where Ultima used to be," he said. "Now it's a rockpile. If they roll up their sleeves and get at it, they ought to be able to dig Yates out of there in about fifty years."

"Ultima," Tracker said, weighing the word in his mind.

"Pretty fancy name for a rockpile, huh?"

"They should have called it Jericho," Tracker said.

From the *New York Daily Tribune* Science Section,
Tuesday, December 10, 1991

IS BALL LIGHTNING REAL? LAB IS IN HOT PURSUIT

by Malcolm W. Browne

For centuries scientists have debated the existence of "ball lightning," a phenomenon thousands of witnesses claim to have seen but that has usually defied scientific investigation.

Two Japanese physicists have reported, however, that they have created glowing discharges suggestive of natural lightning balls, and that these balls can now be studied in the laboratory.

The two, Yoshi-hiko Ohtsuki of Waseda University and H. Ofuruton of Tokyo Metropolitan College of Aeronautical Engineering, said they had built a microwave device that creates glowing, lightning-like globes that float in air and exhibit many of the properties attributed to ball lightning. They described their research in the current issue of the British journal *Nature*. . . .

Afghanistan: August, 1986

The name Hindu Kush meant "Hindu Killer." The Pathan tribes who lived in this forboding mountain wilderness called it *Bam-i-Dunya*, the Roof of the World. To Tony Gallio, the terrain seemed majestically surreal in its savage beauty, a rock-strewn, broken landscape of jagged, twenty thousand-foot peaks that seemed to stretch into infinity. Rushing torrents of ice-cold snowmelt roared through its steep defiles. Twisted scrub pines and cedar trees grew out of nearly vertical rock walls. The days were mercilessly hot. The nights were bitingly cold. It was a brutal, unforgiving land that had defied the armies of Darius the Great and Alexander. The hordes of Ghengis Khan and Tamerlane had stormed through its precarious mountain passes, but had ultimately failed to conquer it. The British Empire had experienced some of its worst defeats here, humbled by the untamed land and its indomitable people. And now the Soviets were floundering in this fierce and primitive country, throwing everything they had against the freedom fighters of Afghanistan and failing to subdue them. The Hindu Kush killed those who did not belong here.

Tony Gallio was no stranger to harsh, inhospitable country. He had survived the steaming jungles of Vietnam and Cambodia. He had slogged through the dense undergrowth of Nicaragua. He had returned unscathed from covert missions in such places as El Salvador and Lebanon, but he had never before encountered country quite like this. The rocky path they followed was barely a foot wide, with a sheer drop of several thousand feet directly to his left. One false step could prove fatal. Despite being in superb physical condition, Gallio was breathing like a spent marathoner and his clothes were soaked with sweat. It was all he could do to keep up with the seemingly inexhaustable *mujahidin*, the holy warriors of the *Jihad*.

The days stretched into weeks as they continued on their trek. The Panjshir Valley, seventy miles long with an elevation of seven thousand feet, was a three-week journey from the border. Located forty miles to the north of Kabul, it was a valley of mud and stone villages, vineyards, wheat fields and fruit orchards, with one main entry road to the south flanked by steep escarpments. It was controlled by the Russians, inasmuch as they controlled anything in Afghanistan. They had a base there for the Hind helicopter gunships. It was a place that Gallio thought should provide some fine target practice. He was looking forward to shooting one down himself. It was, of course, strictly against orders. He wasn't even supposed to be here. He could imagine what would happen if it ever got out that a colonel in the American Special Forces, working for the CIA, had shot down a Russian helicopter with a Stinger missile. But there was no way he was going to miss this chance.

Along the way, they frequently saw flights of MiGs passing overhead. Several times, they observed groups of four or six helicopter gunships. They remained out of sight, hidden in the rocks, despite the mounting enthusiasm felt by the *mujahidin*, who were anxious to try out the Stingers. They had heard about them, because the forces in Pakistan had been equipped with both Stingers and Sidewinder air-to-air missiles. There were F-16 jet fighters in Pershawar, provided as part of the military aid by the United States, to protect Pakistani airspace and prevent the MiGs from attacking the refugee camps. The temptation to fire on some of the helicopters they saw was great, but it was essential not to give themselves away before they reached their destination. To ease the tension somewhat, Gallio unpacked one of the Stingers and gave them dry run instructions in its use, all without ever actually firing it. Soon, he told them, the time would come when they would get the opportunity to use them.

As they continued on their journey, they encountered several groups of *mujahidin*, as well as Afghan villagers. The people were dirt poor, living in simple, thatch-roofed houses with dirt floors, but their hospitality was always effusive and they shared what little they had. They lived by their code of *Pakhtunwali*, the unwritten laws of social conduct composed of three main dictums. *Melmastia* demanded that anyone who crossed the threshold of their dwelling be treated as an honored guest, even a sworn enemy. *Nanawatai* dictated that asylum must be granted to anyone who sought it and *badal*, the strictest commandment of them all, demanded remorseless revenge, payment in blood for any personal affront. These were people who believed that it was better to die in battle than in bed. A *shahid*, a martyr who was killed in battle, gained admittance through the gates of Paradise. No wonder the Soviets couldn't crush these people. Death held no fear for them and they didn't know the meaning of surrender. They found freedom in death as well as life.

Gallio was unable to keep his group from talking excitedly about the Stinger missiles to those they met on the trail. He tried to caution them, but it was no use. They were like children with new toys. For all he knew, anyone they met could be a spy for the Karmal regime. For that matter, despite all his best efforts, word of what they carried might have leaked out before they had even crossed the border. However, in a very real sense, the operation was no longer his, but theirs. They would get the missiles to Massoud, but if they met the enemy along the way, they'd fight.

They were about five or six days' journey from their destination when they ran into an ambush. A group of Afghans approached them from down the trail, but something in their manner had given them away before they got too close. Whatever it was, Gallio hadn't spotted it, but the others had and almost before he knew what was happening, he found himself in the middle of a firefight. The "Afghans" were Soviet Spetsnaz commandos in disguise.

The *mujahidin* reacted quickly. Half of them rushed forward and took up position to cover the retreat, so the others could escape with their precious cargo of Stingers. But the Russians had prepared for that. The previous night, a flight of helicopters had passed by overhead, an occurence that had become so common, Gallio hadn't paid much attention to it. The choppers had dropped off several squads of commandos to their rear and they had moved up during the night, setting up a hammer-and-anvil assault to hit them from both sides.

As bullets struck the rocks around them, Sikander shouted, *"Boro! Boro!"* ("Let's go! Let's go!") He grabbed Gallio's arm and tried to pull him back out of the way, but Gallio shook him off and took up a position to return the fire with his AK-47, covering the others while they quickly started taking the missiles off the frightened pack animals. They shouldered them and began to scamper up into the rocks like mountain goats. Bullets whined off the rocks around them. Gallio felt a sharp pain as his cheek was lacerated by a stone chipped off by a round from a Kalashnikov. Adrenaline surged through his bloodstream as he returned the fire.

Cries of *"Allah o Akbar!"* and *"Mordabad Shouravi!"* echoed over the sharp, firecracker bursts of the automatic weapons. Then, suddenly, another sound was added to the din as the loud, staccato clatter of helicopter blades filled the air. The Hind helicopter gunships swooped down like screaming pterodactyls, raining a deadly hail of bullets into the moutainside. One of the panicked mules was cut completely in half as the chopper "walked" its fire up the trail and Gallio heard a scream as Sikander's body was reduced to bloody pulp in less than two seconds. He huddled behind the rock outcropping where he had taken shelter, trying to become a part of it as bullets slammed into the mountain all around him, sending dust and stone fragments flying in all directions. Then he heard a loud *whoosh* and a concussive *whump* as the helicopter blossomed into a bright orange fireball.

He glanced up and saw Daoud, the little thirteen-year-old who had paid such close and rapt attention when he had explained the function of the Stingers, lowering the tube from his shoulder, raising his fist and shouting out triumphantly. He had downed the first Soviet helicopter gunship in the Afghan War.

"Awriight!" Gallio shouted, with elation. *"Yeah, Daoud!"*

The boy waved at him, a wide grin on his face. Then his small body jerked convulsively and fell as it was struck by a burst of machine gun fire. Gallio screamed hoarsely as he emptied the magazine of his AK-47 into the commando who had killed the boy. He jacked out the clip and slapped a fresh one in.

But before he could raise the rifle, he felt a sledgehammerlike blow to his head and everything went black.

He woke up to the jouncing of a truck careening down a rutted road. He was lying on a bloodsoaked truckbed, surrounded by the dead bodies of the freedom fighters. The Soviets knew it had a demoralizing effect on the *mujahidin* when they took away the bodies of slain freedom fighters, thereby denying them a Moslem burial.

Gallio was surprised to discover he was still alive. His head was throbbing. The bullet must have only grazed him. He no longer had on his turban, but his head was bandaged. The side of his face felt sticky, but he couldn't tell if it was from his own blood or the sticky gore on the floor of the truckbed. He couldn't raise his hands to feel it. They were tied behind his back. His feet were tied, as well. He was trussed up like a roped calf, a short cord running behind him from his hands to his feet, arching his back painfully. He was hemmed in by bodies and he couldn't move. The stench was awful.

He had no idea how long he had been out. He had no idea what time it was, whether it was day or night. He heard only the roar of the truck's engine and felt the jarring impact as it bounced over the road. He tried to think. There hadn't been a road close to where they were when the ambush had gone down, so they must have carried him out and loaded him onto a chopper, then transferred him to the truck along with the bodies.

"Well, son," he mumbled to himself, "you finally did it. You really screwed the pooch this time."

The truck braked to a stop. He heard doors slamming and the sound of running footsteps. A moment later, the back gate of the truck was lowered and the tarp was pulled aside. Two men jumped up into the truckbed, walking over the bullet-riddled bodies of the *mujahidin*, and Gallio felt himself lifted painfully and tossed out on the ground. He fell on his side and grunted. His head felt like a thousand hangovers. Someone leaned down and cut the cord running from his wrists to his feet, then cut the cord around his ankles.

"Vstavai! Vstavai, svolotch!"

A booted foot connected with his ribs.

Gallio grunted with pain and awkwardly lumbered to his feet. Every muscle in his body felt cramped. It was dusk. The sky was a wild orange-purple as the sun set. The wind blew gently on his face. He was in a valley, possibly the Panjshir, though he had no way of knowing for sure. The mountains rose majestically around him. As he quickly glanced around, he saw large tents and rows of corrugated iron huts. A hundred or so yards in front of him was a supply depot, with several trucks parked alongside it, as well as four BMP armored vehicles with 30 mm cannons. Farther off, he could see a line of BM-21 rocket launchers positioned near the perimeter of the camp, aimed to fire salvos at the mountain slopes. Nearer, there was a line of APCs, a couple of fuel tankers, and a row of T-64 tanks. To his right, there were several rows of Hind-24s, those huge, ugly-looking choppers with stubby wings and weapons pods. Someone gave him a hard shove and he almost lost his footing.

Four men marched him around the front of the truck and the sight was right out of *Gunga Din.* It was a huge adobe fort, with thick, thirty-foot walls and gun towers. A gun barrel prodded his back as he was marched through the large, heavy wooden gates. They marched him down a series of dark and narrow corridors, illuminated by lights strung on wire. He heard someone screaming. They brought him to a room and shoved him inside, then tied him to a wooden chair placed behind a folding table. One of the soldiers struck him hard across the face, drawing blood. Gallio spat at him and received a gun butt in his stomach for his trouble. As he fought to get his breath back, the door opened and a colonel in the sand-colored uniform of the Spetsnaz commandos entered.

He was tall and muscular, with dark, curly hair and deep-set brown eyes. He was about forty years old, deeply tanned, with sharply chisled features. Behind him came another man, a swarthy-looking Afghan in the uniform of the Karmal regime. He came up to Gallio and asked him something in Pushto. Gallio didn't understand a word. He simply stared at his interrogator belligerently. The man struck him in the face and repeated his query. Gallio said nothing.

One of the Russian soldiers raised his rifle to strike Gallio in the face with the gun butt, but the colonel quickly said, *"Nyet!"* and the rifle was lowered. *"Ostavteh nas."*

He jerked his head toward the door and the others left, leaving him alone with Gallio.

He took out a silver cigarette case, snapped it open, took one for himself, then held out the case to Gallio and raised his eyebrows. Gallio nodded. The Russian took one out and placed it between Gallio's lips. He lit it, then lit his own and exhaled the smoke through his nostrils.

"My name is Col. Grigori Andreyvitch Galinov," he said, in excellent, though heavily accented English. "What is your name?"

Gallio gazed at him with an uncomprehending expression and shrugged his shoulders.

"Your pretence at ignorance is pointless," Galinov said, matter-of-factly. "I will ask you again, what is your name?"

Gallio did not reply.

"You know that we can make you talk," Galinov said. "You are, no doubt, familiar with our techniques of interrogation. Why put yourself through unnecessary pain?"

Gallio said nothing.

The Russian officer stared at him thoughtfully. "Very well. You do not wish to tell me your name. In that case, I will try another question."

He leaned forward across the table, close to Gallio's face, staring at him intently. He held up a gold signet ring.

"Where did you get this?"

Gallio recognized his own ring, a gold signet inscribed with the symbol of a *gladius*, the Roman short sword, surrounded by the letters P.B.M.M.G. He had not realized until that moment that they had removed it from his finger. And as the Russian held it up before him, Gallio saw, with a shock, that he was wearing a ring that was absolutely identical.

Galinov saw the expression on his face and his eyes narrowed. He took the cigarette from between Gallio's lips and tossed it aside.

"*Where?*" he repeated.

"It belonged to my great grandfather," said Gallio, staring at him with astonishment. "Where did you get yours?"

"It has been in my family for generations," said Galinov. He placed the ring on the table before Gallio and straightened up. "*Pro bono. . . ?*" he said, watching Gallio with an anxious, intense gaze.

Gallio felt a fist start squeezing his insides. He swallowed hard. "*Pro bono majori, maxima gloria,*" he said, completing the Latin motto that the letters on the ring stood for. He felt suddenly lightheaded.

"So you know the words," Galinov said, slowly. "But who was the first to say them?"

"Marcus Lucius Gallio. My ancestor." He moistened his lips. "And who did he say them to?"

"To Hanno, son of Hannibal," Galinov replied. He exhaled heavily. *"Chiort vazmi!"* he swore, softly. "Who *are* you?"

"Col. Anthony Mark Gallio." Suddenly, it hit him. He couldn't believe it. He felt as if he had been gut-punched. "Gallio? *Galinov*?"

"We are kinsmen," said the Russian, staring at him with awe.

"Jesus Christ! I can't fucking believe it!"

"Your shock is no greater than mine, I assure you," Galinov said. He shook his head. "If this were any other regiment than Spetsnaz, that ring would surely have been stolen."

He took his knife out, went around behind Gallio's chair and cut his bonds. Then he opened the door and called out, *"Suvorov! Prenehsi butilku vodki."*

A few moments later, a sergeant entered with a bottle of vodka and two shot glasses. Galinov nodded and dismissed him. The man left and shut the door. As Gallio massaged his wrists, Galinov opened the bottle and poured them each a shot. "What the devil shall we drink to?" he asked. "You have children?"

"A son."

"I, also. To the children, then."

"To the children," Gallio said, softly. They drank.

"Of all the places in the world to meet," Galinov said, offering Gallio another cigarette. He took it and Galinov lit it for him. "You are Special Forces, of course. Yes, you would be." He snorted and shook his head. "You son of a bitch."

Gallio said nothing. He was still in a daze. Galinov refilled their glasses.

"I had thought that my branch of the family was the last," he said.

"So did I," said Gallio.

"A colonel in the United States Army Special Forces, working for the CIA, of course," Galinov said. He shook his head. *"Yob tvayu maht."*

Gallio had some knowledge of Russian. He was familiar with the Russian equivalent of motherfucker.

Col. Galinov stared at him for a long moment, a strange expression on his face. "What is your son's name?"

"Tony, Jr."

"Mine is Alexei," Galinov said. "He will be six years old now. I have not seen him since he was four."

"Mine's eight."

Galinov nodded. "I hate this lousy war."

"I hate the way you're fighting it," said Gallio.

Galinov nodded again, his gaze distant. "Yes. So do I. This is not a war for soldiers, but for butchers. I can no longer sleep without nightmares. What we are doing here fills me with disgust. May God forgive us."

"God?" said Gallio.

Galinov smiled, wryly. "You are surprised? Did you think that all of us were atheists? I am Russian Orthodox. And when I return home to Novgorod, if I should return, I shudder at the things I must confess."

"Why?" asked Gallio. "Why kill innocent civilians? Why the atrocities, Galinov?"

"The United States has never committed atrocities, I suppose?" Galinov said, sarcastically. "What of your Lt. Calley? What of your support of the Nicaraguan Contras?"

"I won't deny the Contras commit atrocities, but we don't control the Contras and Calley was prosecuted. What he did wasn't our policy, as it is yours. You people are committing genocide."

"And your hands are so clean?" Galinov said. "Your country's history is without blemish? What about your American Indians?"

"That was in the past," Gallio said.

"So shall this be, one day," said Galinov. "But whether you believe it or not, I don't like it any more than you do." He refilled their glasses again. "For the first time, there are demonstrations against the war back home. Such a thing has never been before. Our young people do not wish to go. It is like your Vietnam. They injure themselves to get medical exemptions, some even pretend insanity and go to institutions rather than serve in the army." He shook his head. "There is talk we may be pulling out soon. I hope to God it's true."

He shoved his chair back and got up. His manner seemed to change. He drew himself up and looked down at Gallio. Without warning, he punched Gallio in the face, knocking him back over his chair and breaking his nose. As Gallio struggled back up, Galinov hit him three more times, powerful, punishing blows that bloodied his mouth and cut the skin over his left eye. Gallio collapsed to the floor.

Galinov opened the door and shouted something to the men outside. They came in, picked Gallio up, and took him to a cell. They shoved him in and he fell sprawling on the dirt floor. There were rats crawling in the corners. The door was slammed and bolted.